entertainment

Richard
John
Evans

entertainment

seren

seren is the book imprint of
Poetry Wales Press Ltd
Nolton Street, Bridgend, CF31 3BN, Wales
www.seren-books.com

ISBN 1-85411-287-2

The publisher works with the financial assistance of the
Arts Council of Wales

Printed in Plantin by Gomer Press, Llandysul, Ceredigion

entertainment

1. AUGUST 1993

The Journals of Philip McKay (pronounced Mac-A not Mac-I)

Woke up with C3-PO staring me in the face. Quite freaky – just the head, on a stand next to the anglepoise. Almost expected him to start talking. "Master Philip, I would appreciate it if you would locate my body unit and replace my head. This is quite undignified." Camp as tents. Quite a good model, going cheap at Forbidden Planet in Cardiff. Put batteries in to light up the eyes. I know every line and rivet of his face. Better than most of my family. *Star Wars* was pivotal. Looked so real, so big. A whole generation still waiting for the Millennium Falcon to arrive. Han Solo jumps out. "C'mon kid, let's get moving. The Empire's got a trace on us." Technology takes so long to catch up. And one planet is so restrictive, we need a whole galaxy. Evil Empire to fight, plenty to do, rush to the X-wings.

Up the dole office then, to sign on. Massive queue, heaters turned up too high. Twenty minutes standing by the pot plant, shuffling forward. Endless, pointless spills of conversation.

"How's Mike these days?"

"I don't know, haven't seen him for ages."

"He still with that Suzanne girl?"

"Last time I seen him."

"His father's from Bristol."

"Never to God."

"That's right now."

"I never knew that."

Pause, clear their throats, look around, shuffle forward, and then: "Tell you who I saw the other day – Ken."

"Ken?"

"Ken bins."

"Oh aye."

"He's gone to look old."

"Lost a lot of weight."

"Been ill, haven't he?"

"Oh hell, yeah. Death's door, like."

"Pity. Got a lot of time for old Ken."

"Bit of wanker to his missus,"

"Ken? Yeah, bit of a wanker."

"Smashing bloke, though."

"Ken's all right."

Found out why the queue was so long. People signing off. Big drop in seasonally adjusted figures. Combination of microtechnology and drugs. Big firms come from Japan, set up TV and PC factories. Bigger than towns. M4 corridor. Hidden by screening trees. Got their own effluent lagoons. Take them for duck ponds. So do ducks. Swim on them. Their feet rot. Firms employ thousands, soldering circuits. They love Wales, Sony and the others. We work for peanuts. For peanut shells. For the promise of peanut shells. And so on.

Then drugs. Easy to explain. Little Welsh valley missed the 60s. Too busy digging for coal, cheering on the rugby team. Drugs? I'd rather a pint of bitter and a chorus of *Delilah*. Or whatever. End of the 80s arrives – what now? Pits closed, rugby's crap. Socialism is an Alexei Sayle joke. Someone spots a new market to open up. We turn on, tune in, but have already dropped out. No – been dropped out. New market prised wide open. First dope, then speed, then temazis, diazepam, any old tranks, bit of E, some acid, up the scale to crack and smack. Like the summer of love, but chillier. Massive success. Drugs mean work for all. Finally, a new growth industry.

Between the two there's no need for anyone under thirty to claim benefit anymore. Busy fingers all around the valley. The TV-makers can afford a car at last and the drug dealers nick it. Sell it on. Some other solderer buys it for a good price. Replaces the one he had nicked last week. And so on. Thriving economy once more. Me, I stay out of both markets. No idealism, just lazy. Lazy and sick and ill. Etc etc. White boy angst. Nice line in cynicism, GCSE in computers, very little else.

Skinny, spotty kid, former school mate, signs off, passes me on the way out.

"Sony?" I say.

"Nah, mate." Grins. "Wouldn't work there if you paid me."

Drugs, then. Nice work. No downsizing to worry about, total quality initiatives, teamwork exercises, investors in people. Threat of prison almost unreal. Only problem – obligatory mobile phones get bad signals in the valley. I sometimes climb up the mountain, walk along the old tram line, with my scanner. Stand on rugged precipice and pick up conversations.

"Seen Ricky?"

"Not since Friday."

"He got some stuff."

"He's a bit of a wanker."

"He's all right, Ricky."

"See you down the Feathers."

"About half eight."

"Later."

Walk through leafy glades and so on, listening to Radio Four, while sheep run frightened into ferns.

So – signed on, walked out into the brilliant morning. Only get to see one morning every two weeks. Appreciate them more. Past the river, back to the house. Think about Jason, last time we went for a drink. In some Cardiff pub. People very friendly. A man referred to Jason's wheelchair as a chariot. Big mistake. Pet hate of Jason's. The vertical line between his eyebrows suddenly deepened, like an exclamation mark. Screamed abuse, offered them outside. One guy was up for it, but a bit squeamish about fighting a paraplegic. Jason introduced him quite forcefully to the contents of his pint glass. Then laughed – always the laugh. There was a scuffle. Got thrown out. Jason shouting for more. Went down Caroline Street for chips, Jason laughing his head off. Before, he'd been in a bit of a mood. Afterwards, quite chirpy.

Back to bed. Enough of the brilliant morning. Another one in two weeks. Snuggling down, I kissed C3-PO on his slit-mouth. It was still only eleven. Imagined Jason, at that moment, waking up in his flat. Vivid, forceful. A vision. As if actually seeing it. Went like this.

The bastard sun shoots a hot dose in his eyes. He's not really awake and doesn't want to be. As fucked as his head is he can still work out exactly what is going on. The gap in the curtains, the position of his body on the mattress meeting that of the sun up in the sky – it's just another quick prank, to welcome him to the day, show him he's not forgotten.

Turns on to other side. Still hoping sleep will return. Head starts throbbing. Stomach kicks in. Awake less than a minute and thinking about his first drink. Some days are worse than others, and he has no control over that, none. Days are planned and designed elsewhere.

Awake properly now, and he's got an erection. Against all odds it's particularly impressive this morning. Some paraplegics are impotent. Not Jason. If only. He thinks: my own prick is taking the piss. Tries to ignore it, rolls over. It throbs against his stomach. It's really huge, straining at the leash and so on. Imagines the billions of sperm, gagging to get out. All he can offer is the same as usual – a quick one off the wrist.

Desperate urge to masturbate runs alongside desperate urge not to masturbate. Unless there's something to think about, it will turn into a marathon wank. Hammering away until his arm goes dead. Just wants it over with, so he doesn't have to think about sex until the day is over. Can't face trawling through a catalogue of increasingly depraved images, looking for something to excite the jaded hormones, only to fall back on Claire. Claire Louise McKay. My sister.

Looks around. Ripped mattress on the floor of a dirty flat. Drunk cripple lying on it, wanking into his own fag ash and spilt booze. Doesn't want to drag Claire into this. Leaves himself alone.

Awake for eight minutes now. Each one more miserable than the last. Some days are better than this. Wakes at midday, slowly. Gets breakfast – solid, not booze. Watches daytime TV. Sometimes spends a whole day blank, even without booze, until the evening anyway. But today is one of those ones – eight minutes of consciousness, eight minutes of misery.

Shouldn't even be awake, for fuck's sake. Eleven o'clock. Wide awake now, can't find no sleep left in his brain to slide into. Mind alert and active, with nothing to think about but his own miserable shitty life as the world's oldest surviving abortion. Body's awake too – head and cock throbbing counterpoint, back of his throat begging him to splash alcohol all over it, genetically wasted legs screaming for their morning fix. Nine minutes into the day and the whole lot's awake and screaming.

Doesn't bother ringing the support group to tell them he's not coming in. Probably have a party. No-one to disrupt the therapeutic chats. Looks around the room for his chair. Miles away. Fuck it. Starts crawling to the cabinet. Bottle of vodka in there. Not much left. Enough, though. Covers the distance quite quickly. Props himself up on his arms. Like doing press-ups. Or shagging.

Crawls over leather jacket, past Pot Noodle tubs doubling as ashtrays, plates with remains of last night's Chinese and towers of teabags, wank mags, book of Beckett plays I lent him which he hasn't read, Nurofen boxes, ripped Nirvana poster and so on.

He can move his legs. Sometimes tries to walk. Too weak to hold him up. Don't do what he wants them to. Blockage somewhere. Not fixable. Crawling, he wriggles the legs. Extra traction. Other than that, he might as well have a pair of paper streamers attached to his belt.

Reaches the cabinet, sticks an arm in, out falls a letter from Claire. The latest one. Apologies and please come back. He thinks: thanks for that, cheers. Another little jape there. On form this morning. Then, of course: Should he ring her? Doesn't know what to do about her. Or me. Are we his responsibility? His fucking children? He sighs or grunts. Weariness or disgust. I never know which.

Drops the letter, gets the vodka. Not much left. Pours it down throat. Slumps and rests. Booze goes down. Burns when it hits stomach. Just shows it's working. Best medicine. Sits with back against cabinet, lets it soak in. Sun pouring through curtains, everything lit up, the crap all over the room. Takes another drink. Phone rings. Crawls to coffee table, picks it up.

"Hello?" Trying to sound suave, in case it's Claire.

"Is that Jason?"

"Yeah."

"Hiya Jase, it's Martin. How's it going?"

"All right." Starts looking for fags.

"We were just wondering if you were coming in today, so I thought I'd give a ring."

"Yeah, no. No, I'm giving it a miss today."

"Oh right, fair enough," Martin says.

Finds the fags. Starts looking for a light.

"Are you ill?" Martin asks.

"Well, of course I'm fucking ill, Martin. We're all ill. That's the point of the group, isn't it? Or is there some other common denominator between us all? Something I've missed? Hang on a minute." Jason slides under the table, grabs his lighter, comes back to the phone. "Sorry, Mart, had to get my lighter."

"Listen, Jase, why don't you pop down, we can have a chat."

"Nah, you're all right mate. I'll just stick around here for a bit."

"Have you got that flu that's going around?"

"No. But I'm a cripple, if that's any help."

"You don't sound very happy at the moment."

"No?"

"You're not, are you?"

"Oh, Martin, I don't want to burden you. I don't want you to think I'm being self-indulgent, Martin."

Nice long pause. Martin tries to work out if Jason is taking the piss.

Finally: "Don't be funny, Jason. We're all in the same boat."

"Boat? I'm not in a boat. What the fuck are you talking about?"

Jason, in my mind, throws down some more vodka. My best friend in the world is starting to wake up now.

"Look, some days I just want to have a bloody good moan," Martin says. "We all do."

"But there's a difference between us, isn't there?"

"And what's that, Jason?"

"You're physically challenged. I'm a cripple."

He can hear Martin breathe out, away from the phone.

12

Grins. Teeth clenched. Ready for the kill. All he needs is Martin's next line.

"It's the same for all of us, Jason. It doesn't matter what words you use. It's the same for all of us."

Jason pushes himself up, hunches over the phone. The line between his eyebrows, his exclamation mark, deepens.

"Yeah, but I look at it different, see." His thuggish voice now. "You all go to fucking Parliament, kick up a fuss about wheelchair access, all that bollocks, and I don't give a shit about any of it. I don't give a finger-fuck for the disabled."

"Yes, but Jason, it's about attitude, how you approach –"

"Listen, listen, just listen," Jason hisses. "I don't get angry about what you get angry about. You get angry about the disabled not having proper resources. I get angry about being the fucking disabled. And that's the fucking boat I'm in, Martin."

"Jason, all I'm saying is that there's no point getting angry about things you can't change. It's about finding a way for you, yourself, to deal with it."

"I don't want to fucking deal with it. I want to, well, let's see, walk for a start. Be able to go for a shit without planning it for half an hour beforehand. Kick some fucker in the head. You know, the normal things."

His big arms are bulging now. Vein in his neck throbbing. He's getting into it.

"Look, Jason, why don't you come down, just for an hour? We're all here, no-one's going to –"

"Martin, listen, just answer the following question: do you reckon it's fair?"

"God, we've been through this before, Jason, it gets you nowhere."

"Yeah, but just to humour me, answer yes or no."

"To prove what point? The whole notion of fairness –"

"Yes or no?"

"It's neither fair nor unfair. It's time for you to grow up, Jason."

"Fucking bollocks, complete shit, useless," Jason gabbles down the phone. "You think this is all accident, it's not, nothing is. You can't see any further than the coffee machine down the hall. Good luck to you, not that you need it. Hey, Martin, I can hear the doorbell. I've got to go now."

"Will we see you on Thursday?"

"Who knows? Not me, that's for sure. Christ alone knows. Go to go. Have a nice day, yeah?"

"Uh-huh. See you,"

"Bye."

Phone down. Collapses on to the floor. Reaches for the cushion. Under his head. Wriggles, gets comfortable. Stretches, grabs remote control. TV on. Makeover in progress. Grabs booze and fags. Relaxes. Thinks: Nice chat with Martin. Woken me up a bit.

Camera pans back, takes in whole room, Jason lying on the floor. Fade to black. Vision ends. So vivid. As if I were there. Heard every word, Martin's voice down the phone. Jason's face, his movements. My best friend in the world, waking to a new day. I pull the duvet from my shoulders. Too warm.

2. AUGUST 1990.

While Philip slept, the sun came out again. It was such a dull, grey day he came inside and started to read his book on the making of the *Star Wars* films. He dozed off during a detailed account of the way the final assault on the Death Star had been filmed, and then the sun came out. By this time, mid afternoon, the sun had moved almost over the top of the caravan, but one ray made it inside, through the frosted pane at the upper edge of the side window. It landed on Philip's upper arm, creating a brilliant three inch yellow patch on his pale skin. The bubbled glass magnified it, and Philip woke suddenly, the patch tingling. He held his arm up and looked at it, then a gnat flew into his eye and he started rubbing it. Soon, the gnat was free and the skin around his eye hurt, while the patch on his arm began to sting. He could hear his father outside, playing the guitar. He leaned his head against warm formica and looked at the last segment of sun, smeared over the frosted glass. He imagined himself shrunk, almost microscopic, travelling at vast speed through the rivulets in the pane. All around him glowed yellow, like the crazy-paved surface of the sun. A semi-erection pulsed lazily in his jeans as he raced along the luminous corridors.

Later, he joined his family for a walk over to the harbour.

"If you ask me, Caernarfon's got it all," Val, his father, said. "Lovely harbour, lovely castle, lovely pubs and a lovely caravan site. I don't know why people bother going abroad."

"Well, it's the weather, isn't it?" Joan, his mother, said.

"No, it's not that," Val grinned. "Look at Phil, here. This is probably the last year he'll come on holiday with us. Next year he'll be off with a load of his mates to the Costa whatever, and we all know why. Not that I can blame him. Just wish I was his age again." He laughed and Joan gave him a tap on the arm.

"Ignore him," she said.

Claire, Philip's sister, said, "He hasn't got any mates,

15

anyway. They all go to the pub but they won't let him in because he's so skinny."

"That's right, because there's a weight restriction on buying booze, isn't there?" Philip said.

"There is as far as you're concerned," Claire said.

"I don't know why everyone makes so much fuss about drinking," Joan said. "You can have just as much fun without it."

"That reminds me," Val said. "Looks like I've got a regular spot at the King's when we go back." He bent down to correct a minor flaw in his left flip-flop. "I'll have to expand the old repertoire a bit though. Any ideas?"

"*Summertime Blues*," Philip grunted.

"Yeah. A bit of rock and roll." Val said. "Good call, Phil." He started to sing the song, tapping out time on his wife's bag. "*I'm gonna take my girlfriend to the United Nations*," he sang.

"Girlfriend?" Philip said.

"Yeah, that's right, isn't it?"

"I think it's 'problem', actually." He stopped to tie his shoelace and muttered, "Why the fuck would Eddie Cochran want to take his fucking girlfriend to the United fucking Nations, for fuck's sake?"

"Such a limited vocabulary," Claire said, peering down at him.

"When you're older," Philip said, "you'll come to realise that certain swear words correspond exactly to certain life experiences, and that this is why they exist. Until then, why don't you –"

He straightened up and whispered in her ear.

"And you wonder why you haven't got a girlfriend," she said.

Claire leaned on the railings, brushed her hair from her eyes and gazed across the marina. Philip slouched beside her, letting himself be dazzled by sun, split by the water from a single star into a constellation.

"There's some people over there waving at us," Claire said.

"Where, over there?" Val said. "Waving at us?"

Philip looked up. "Yeah, see them? They're definitely waving at us," he said.

Claire waved.

"Hang on," Val said. "Joan, where's my glasses?"

His wife fished them from her bag, and Val looked again.

"Well, I'll be buggered," he said.

Claire sniggered, still waving. Unnoticed, her bracelet fell off her wrist.

"It's Ryan and Elaine, I think," Val said, heading for the gang plank that led to the yachts.

"Who are they?" Claire asked.

"Old friends of ours. Your father was in school with Ryan. We used to go on double dates," Joan said.

They had all drifted in Val's wake to a small gate at the entrance to the marina, ready to meet the old friends. They clustered around, but the gate was blocked by a teenager in a wheelchair. He had dark, spiky hair and sat where he was, ignoring them. The old friends were crossing the gangplank, getting closer, waving the whole time. The boy still blocked the gate. It was getting a little awkward, and Philip backed off. The boy looked the McKays up and down, then looked away. Val turned to him and opened his mouth to speak, but Ryan had arrived. He ignored the gate and climbed over the railing. His wife, carrying two bags and a jacket, followed awkwardly.

"Christ almighty, you old sod," Val said.

"Hey, less of the old," Ryan said, taking off his baseball cap. "I'm not the one going grey."

"At least I've got some hair to go grey."

Philip realised that he formed part of a semi-circle, along with Claire, his mother, Ryan's wife and the ignorant boy in the wheelchair. The two men were in the centre and the shape was sealed by the harbour railings. He watched his father and Ryan shake hands. First Val held out his right hand to Ryan, who took it with both his hands. Then Val put his other hand on top of the whole construction and they both clasped. Finally, they shook. Ryan had propped his baseball cap on a balustrade and Philip read what was written on it: *Canadian Air Force Bomber Command.*

When he looked up, his mother and Elaine had their arms around each other, and each was smiling over the other's shoulder, into the air.

"Well, well, well," Ryan said.

"Fancy that," Joan said.

"I thought it was all foreign holidays for you these days," Val said.

Philip noticed Ryan and Elaine exchange a quick glance, then noticed everyone else noticing it.

"Well, you've got to come back sometimes, haven't you?" Ryan said. "And we've got the boat here." He pointed across the marina.

"That's yours, is it?" Val said, shading his eyes.

"Well, ours and some friends'." Ryan said.

"Best thing you ever did was move."

"How long has it been now?" Joan asked.

"Well, we went to Leicester in '66," Elaine said, "but we've seen you since then, haven't we?"

"Yeah, when this one was born," Val said, reaching out to pat Philip's shoulder.

Philip moved to the left and his foot bumped against a wheel. The disabled boy was still there. He grinned at Philip, then up at the reunion. A vertical line appeared between his eyebrows.

"So who do you play for, son?" Ryan said.

"Pardon?"

"Rugby," Ryan said. "Don't you play?"

"No, he's more of a bookworm, this one," Val said.

"Looks like you'd be good on the wing, though," Ryan said."Is he fast?"

"Fast enough when there's some work to be done," Val said.

"I bet. Kids."

"This is it."

Philip watched the two men open their mouths very wide and, a split second later, laugh.

"And you must be Claire, are you?" Elaine said, and Claire nodded. "How old are you, Claire?"

"I'm eleven now but I'll be twelve in two months."

"Haven't you got lovely hair," Elaine stroked Claire's fringe. "And what do you want to do when you get older?"

18

"I'd like to be a theatre director, and perhaps a theatre manager with a tremendous influence on British drama, like they used to be in the old days," Claire said.

Philip smiled. Heard it all before, it was her script.

"I know it's going to involve a lot of menial work backstage in the regional theatres, but I'm really looking forward to giving it a go," she said.

Hiding his smile, Philip turned it away from the reunion and ended up grinning at the boy in the wheelchair. He was now staring at Claire, who noticed and turned to face him. Suddenly, they were all looking at him, as he sat fiddling with something he held in his right hand.

"You've met our boy already, then?" Ryan said. "Or hasn't he said hello yet?"

Ryan reached past Philip's shoulder and pulled the wheelchair out of the semi-circle and into the centre, where he and Val still stood.

"This is Jason," Ryan said.

He sat looking out at them, chewing gum and breathing through his nose. His eyes were as dark as his hair. He was handsome, square-jawed and manly.

"Say hello to everyone, Jase," Elaine said.

"Hello everyone," Jason said. His voice was deep and flat.

"Hiya, old mate, Val said. "Last time I saw you, you were wearing nappies."

"I still do," Jason said, but everyone pretended not to have heard him.

He was not grinning, Philip decided, but sneering. It was amazing how easy he made it look. For Philip, the sneer was the trickiest of all expressions to pull off. He had only tried it in the mirror so far, and it made him look as though he had an ulcer.

Val nudged him, and he stepped forward into the centre.

"All right, mate?" Philip said.

"Do I look all right?" Jason shrugged.

There was an intake of breath somewhere behind them, and Philip stepped back into the semi-circle.

Then, Claire stepped forward.

"What's your handicap?" she said, standing in front of Jason.

Jason looked her up and down, then beckoned her closer with his right hand. Something swung from his fingers. He was holding the bracelet Claire had dropped. It was made of six beads which spelled out her name.

"Well, C.L.A.I.R.E.," Jason said, "why don't you have a guess?" He swung the bracelet in front of her.

She watched it move. They were very close now.

"Claire –" Joan said.

"No, it's all right," Ryan boomed. He turned to Claire and said, "Jason's legs don't work so he can't walk."

They hadn't moved.

"So how do you go upstairs?" Claire asked, and made a grab for the bracelet.

"I don't," Jason said, letting it go. "There's nothing up there."

And then they were all laughing, slapping each other's backs, Ryan sweeping his baseball cap back on to his head. Philip looked at his sister, her green eyes still fixed on Jason, who stared back with a crooked smile for a second more, then raised his eyes to the sky.

The two families spent the evening in a beer garden. Val and Ryan sang old songs in two-part harmony. Then they got Claire to do her party piece, a recitation from her book of great theatrical speeches. Jason watched her do her Joan of Arc with a puzzled look on his handsome face.

"She always does that," Philip said. "Stupid, isn't it?"

"Want to see my party piece?" Jason said and ruined one of his father's best anecdotes by letting out a series of increasingly loud and polysyllabic belches.

Philip found it very amusing and turned to congratulate Jason, but he had gone. Much later, when they were walking back to the caravan, Philip saw him. He was sitting on his own near a bottle bank, looking out across the bay. His silhouette took a long drink from a bottle, then threw it in the sea.

The next day, they all went to see the castle, even Jason. They plodded around the grounds for an hour, Jason's chair bumping over stones and grass. He looked tired and, when he thought no-one was watching, his head would loll on his big shoulders. He looked up once, saw Philip watching him, and calmly returned the gaze, not sneering, just tired.

Then they came to to the turret, and it started.

"Let's go to the top."

"Yes, there's a lovely view."

"But Jason –"

"You could do a bit of Shakespeare here, Claire."

"Can't we carry him up?"

"What, in the chair?"

"No, we couldn't get it around the spiral."

"But it's a lovely view, from the top."

"We could take him out of the chair, carry him up."

"What do you think, Jase?"

"Would you like that, love? Want us to try to carry you up?"

"No. You go. Leave me here."

They all fell back. His voice could do that, even then. But they started to re-group.

"We can't just leave you, love."

"It's OK, I'll stay with him."

"No, you go, I'll stay. We haven't had chance for a chat yet."

"Well, how about we both stay?"

"No, go on you."

Jason's eyes flicked up, caught Philip's, locked on. Philip hadn't seen him look like this. The arrogance was gone. He looked serious, more serious than Philip could imagine. He kept staring, and Philip's arm rose up, wavered stupidly in the air, the palm outstretched, pointing at Jason. Jason gave a tiny nod, not breaking the stare. Then, Philip was moving, covering the distance between them, looking now at the ground.

"Excuse me, sorry, can I just –? Cheers. Excuse me, thanks," he said, worming his way through them.

"Won't be a minute, sorry to bother you," he said and clasped the handles of Jason's wheelchair.

The parents scattered. Claire had already stood aside. With a shove, he got the chair moving, bumping over the grass and on to the gravel path. He saw Jason's hands gripping the arms of his chair, but he said nothing. Then they were off, picking up speed as they headed towards the drawbridge, Philip fighting an urge to scream obscenities.

They came to a stop in a pub car-park, and Philip slumped to the ground. Breathing heavily, he leaned back against the chair. The spokes dug into his back. He noticed a wasp buzzing around the mouth of a Coke can lying on the ground. Perhaps he shouldn't have done that. Perhaps Jason shouldn't have shocks. He could have a heart condition, brittle bones, God knows, anything. Philip got up and turned to see Jason casually lighting a cigarette.

"Well, that was bracing," Jason said.

They both looked back along the road at the castle. Then Jason held his cigarettes out to Philip. His arm was big, muscular. If he clenched his fist, the cigarette packet would disappear. Crushed. Philip shook his head.

"I don't smoke," he said.

Jason nodded, smiling, and the breeze ruffled his hair.

"I bet you get pissed off with parents and that," Philip said.

Jason's eyes narrowed. He shook his head slowly, the cigarette burning between his lips.

"No, not them," he said, looking over Philip's shoulder. "They're just puppets, aren't they?"

Philip's eyes widened. He leaned closer.

Jason took a long, slow drag on his cigarette, then took his time blowing the smoke out between gritted teeth.

"It's God I can't fucking stand," he said at last.

Philip nodded slowly. "Yeah, God's a bastard."

Jason suddenly grinned at him. Not quite his full sneer though.

That night, Philip left the beer garden with Jason. He marched alongside as Jason wheeled himself along the streets, speeding up when people got in the way. They came to an off-licence.

"Right, Phil, you're under orders," Jason said. "Stay outside."

Philip watched through the window as Jason took his time choosing, then glided up to the counter with a two litre bottle of cider and a six pack of lager. He hoisted them up. The woman looked at them, then down at Jason, then started pressing buttons on her till. She put the cans and bottle in a bag and handed them to Jason, smiling warmly the whole time. Finally, turning to move off, Jason gave her a quick grin.

"It takes a brave shopkeeper to ask a cripple his age," he said as they set off down the street. "I haven't come across one yet."

They stopped at Jason's favourite place, next to the bottle bank. He put his brakes on and sat looking out to sea, the bottle between his legs. Philip circled a few times, glancing around, then sat down. A breeze swept in, cooling them, and Philip let his head loll back, breathing in the air. He saw Jason looking down at him, the bottle in his hand.

"That's right, Phil, enjoy it while you can," he said. "This is what night time's for. They can't get you so easily then." He smiled, showing his teeth.

"Who can't?" Philip said, taking the bottle.

"I'll tell you later, when you've had a few," Jason said.

By midnight Philip was clinging to Jason's chair. The lights in the harbour had turned from sharp points to brilliant streaks across the sky.

"How long have you been like this?" Philip said, tilting his head slowly from side to side, balancing the light show against his nausea.

"Like what?" Jason asked, and they laughed for an hour, and Philip didn't know why.

"Listen, Phil," Jason said. "If I'm a cripple, which I certainly am, and I'm young, which again I confess I am, and 100 per cent sound in the brain department, which I consistently claim to be, then what, I wonder, would you expect my wheelchair to look like?"

"What? A wheelchair, obviously."

"No shit. But in terms of its appearance, my young friend, you would not be too far off the mark to think in terms of one of them fucking customised ones, you know? With the arms cut off and those big plastic things with day-glo sporty shit on stuck over the wheels, hiding the spokes. And stickers advertising Fat Willie's Surf Shack, Penzance on every available fucking surface. And I myself would wear those

23

gloves Tour de France riders wear, leather with no fingers. Are you with me?"

"Oh, yeah, yeah," Philip said, and burped.

"Well, at that point, armed with my sexy, sporty chair and, of course, my positive mental attitude, do you know what I would do? I would compete in the wheelchair Olympics, or the Paralympics, to give them their official title."

"Yeah, you would, yeah."

"But I don't, I smoke fags and I drink booze, and do you know why?"

"Why?"

"Because," Jason said, "they don't do the fucking long jump. And that's the only event I'd fancy having a go at. I've got the knack. Watch this."

He threw the cider bottle into Philip's lap, then reversed his chair crazily down the pavement.

"Check it out," he said.

He came hurtling toward Philip, picking up speed, his arms pumping. Philip rolled out of his way, heard the crash, and turned. Jason was sprawled on the ground. His chair was on its side a few feet away, one wheel spinning. Philip scurried over to him.

"And that, Phil, is why I won't compete in the wheelchair Olympics," Jason said.

Philip shook his head, which seemed ready to fall off its pivot.

"What the fuck did you do that for?" Philip said. "What are you trying to do?"

"Don't take it so seriously," Jason said, struggling upright. "It's all in fun, all in the name of entertainment. Help me up, eh?"

Philip reached out, put his arms around Jason and tried to lift him. He was too heavy and they struggled in the shadow of the bottle bank, their faces almost touching. After a few minutes, Jason was in a sitting position, resting his back against the bottle bank. Philip sat next to him, out of breath. He couldn't stop looking at Jason. The shadow on his face was just right, it highlighted his hard, handsome features. And Jason

24

never stopped looking like himself, never allowed a stray expression cross his face, never a vacant stare or an uncertain wince.

"You're an atheist, I suppose, Phil?" Jason said.

"Yeah, course."

"Well, listen, I just wish you were fucking right, you know? Then you wouldn't have Him doing all this shit, making you do the dance." He trailed off, looked away.

"What dance?" Philip said.

"The stupid, ugly, fucking laughable comedy dance. He leads you on, right, makes you have to do these things, all these fucking things you do, right?"

"What things?"

"All of them. Whatever. Listen, you end up doing all this ridiculous shit, He won't leave you alone just to do nothing, and you look really funny to Him. Can you imagine how amusing you look to Him? From that distance? Fucking amusing indeed. See, He makes you dance around, like, with this stupid miserable look on your face while you do it. And that's the best bit, see, that's what makes it real comedy – your body's doing this childish, ridiculous fucking clown's dance while your face is looking really miserable. That's comedy, Phil."

There was a gleam in his eyes. Philip watched him take another drink and, although he sat quiet while it went down, he knew there was more to come, Jason hadn't finished yet.

"He'll do it to you, too, Phil, and your parents and your sister. Oh yeah, He does it to every fucker. But what He loves most of all, I reckon, is watching the cripples do it. You know what I mean? We can't even dance properly and we look even more miserable, so it's even funnier. Really fucking funny, really fucking mature."

He stopped then and lit up a cigarette. Philip stayed quiet, in case there was more. The dance, he thought, the dance. He could see it. Gnats flew in your eye, the sun burnt a small patch on your arm. It was the same as Jason, just a different scale. You weren't left alone to do nothing, he was right, at least not often enough. But here they were now, he and Jason,

25

hiding behind the bottle bank. They were free, for now at least. He turned to Jason, who was smiling at him, cool and ironic now.

"Here endeth the fucking lesson," Jason said, and giggled.

After that night, the days of the holiday dissolved to nothing, just a splash of yellow between the dark hours spent crouching next to Jason's chair. On the last night, two girls spotted them skulking there. Attracted by the cigarettes and alcohol, they came over. Jason gave them cider and fags, let them take turns with his Walkman. He flirted with them, flexing his big arms at them. He drew them closer, they leaned on his chair. Philip watched, walking around, leaning on the wall, stretching his long legs out on the floor. But it was Jason they were interested in.

He kept flirting but suddenly flared up. The girls would punch him on the shoulder when he was being particularly ballsy, but they always drew back. They were afraid of something, but it wasn't violence. So he dared them to ask what was wrong with him. They did and he tried to convince them he was a lunatic, thrashing and ranting. It got too much for them and they ran off. He watched them go, wiped the drool from his chin and had a fag. Philip stood, with wide eyes, and the silence between them became embarrassing. So Jason gave him a wink and a grin.

"Well, that was entertaining," he said.

Their car was packed. They were ready to go. The sun burned into Philip's head. His hair felt so hot it might ignite. He was hungover. That was something he had Jason to thank for. The two families gathered outside the caravan.

"Let's not leave it so long now," Joan said.

"Well, it probably won't be," Elaine said.

"Come on now," Ryan coughed.

"What?" Elaine said, sharp.

"Nothing," Ryan said.

Philip tried to follow the subtext but his head was too fuzzy. He wasn't noticing much. Jason grinned over at him, dishev-

elled but very handsome. Roguish. Philip wondered how tall
Jason was. Upright. Had he ever stood up? Without the chair,
he'd be unbeatable. If he still had that outlaw cool. But surely
he only had that because of the chair? Or would he be like that
anyway? It was too difficult to work out.

Philip got in the car, looked back at Jason, who gave him a
grin.

"See you, mate," he said, then they were gone.

3. November 1991.

Philip clambered through the railings and sat with his legs crossed on the pillar. Six feet below him the river trickled under the bridge. Six feet behind him the railway track buzzed with the sound of a far-off train carrying home the day's commuters. There was something on Philip's mind but he couldn't bring it out into the light. So he decided to do his trick, his meditation technique. He started by gazing down at the river, noticing the pram stuck in the middle, and acknowledged the fact that this pissy little stream was what had carved out the entire Rhondda valley in the first place. Then he moved up the bridge's main support to the railings, travelling swiftly along the network of indentations and abrasions, briefly noting the industrial revolution and its social and geological upheavals.

The burnt out car in the field was next, and he speculated on the cause of its demise, creating six notional characters along the way. Then he was on to the valley wall, and the streets running in horizontal strips along it. He noted a small playground in between two terraces, and visualised the melted swings, the textualised roundabout, the carpet of broken glass.

There were the allotments then, where the men went to be on their own, and he could see the musty pigeon sheds, full of rusty scythes, unlicensed shotguns and German pornography.

Then there was just the mountain; grass, trees, grass, then rock. He was now gazing at the sky, as out of it as any stoned hippy.

And, on cue, it came to him, what had been on his mind. A question, two in fact. What was the mistake he had made, and when had he made it? After all, he had just turned seventeen, had left school with one GCSE instead of the projected nine, and here he was sitting alone on a railway bridge in Ystrad staring at the sky.

Basically, schematically, it was like this: his good friends at school had mainly done great at their exams, and they were now hanging around the sixth form common room arguing about the political commitment of U2.

His other friends, the ones who did badly, got jobs as pub bouncers, furniture upholsterers and office clerks. Philip, on the other hand, was wandering around the valley looking at things. So where was the mistake? He believed there was a niche for everyone, as the school Dungeons and Dragons Society had proved. So his mistake must be, then, to either have overlooked his own niche, or to have not found it yet, in which case it wasn't a mistake, just circumstance.

For the moment, though, it was pleasant just to go around the place, checking things out. It was still mild, and he spent afternoons lying on his back in quiet parks near technical colleges and factory units. He could gaze at the council estate perched high on the hillside with its streetlights on all day. He could watch tiny cars race along the new road, the valley's best chance to overtake, and listen to them beep at each other. By the time the sound reached him, all impatience and frustration had been drained from it.

Tonight he would go over the King's to watch his father play. He'd gained a regular Friday slot there. It was interesting, watching his father play rock and roll to a room full of pensioners. Philip stretched his legs over the edge of the bridge and leaned back on the pillar. Everything was interesting, in an infinite sort of way. Surely, if he kept wandering around, checking everything out, that elusive niche would open up to him. There was no need to worry, yet. He yawned and relaxed.

At around seven Philip was wandering through Pentre. He went over to the Phoenix Film Theatre and noticed they were showing *The Maltese Falcon*. It cost two quid, so he went in. It was a 60-seater cinema, tucked away in the back of a crumbling old building. They used it as some sort of community centre. He enjoyed the film, except for some bloke with an English accent who kept commenting on it to his friend.

He started the walk home. A bus pulled up opposite the freezer centre so he got on. The journey back to Treorchy took about ten minutes and he hopped off by Saint Dunstan's church. He stopped for chips, then turned the corner into his street. He stuck his key in the door, thinking of Bogart coming up behind Peter Lorre without him knowing, and laying him out with a punch.

There were voices from the living room, not his parents, not Claire. He tiptoed through the passage in the dark, the chip paper rustling and spoiling the effect. He eased open the door to the middle room and stood listening. It sounded familiar. A posh voice. Middle class, but with a trace of Welsh in the vowels. A tendency to pronounce the letter O to rhyme with door, rather than low. He'd heard it before. Definitely. Think. One, two, three, four – Jason's mother, Elaine.

"...with my parents."

"For how long?"

"Until I find a place of my own."

"Anywhere in mind?"

"Well, somewhere around there."

"So, back to Cardiff then."

"Yes. Back to square one."

Philip sauntered into the room. Elaine and Joan were on the settee, and there was Jason, in his chair, by the television.

"Hello, love," Joan said. "We've got visitors."

"Hello Philip, how's it going?" Elaine said.

"I'm all right, yeah," Philip said. "Hiya Jase."

"Any chance of a chip?" Jason said.

Philip walked over and held the bag out to him.

"So what brings you to Wales, then?" Philip asked.

"There's no vinegar on these," Jason growled.

"I don't like vinegar."

"Just visiting," Elaine said.

"Been somewhere nice, Phil?" Joan asked.

"Went to see a film. *The Maltese Falcon.*"

"Oh, your father loves Bogart, doesn't he Jason?" Elaine said.

"Loves the man. Adores him," Jason said.

"This English bloke kept talking," Philip said.

"Yes," Elaine said, "they do that."

"Are you going over the King's Arms tonight?" Joan asked.

"Yeah, thought I'd pop in."

"Why don't you take Jason with you?"

"Yeah, I could do with a drink," Jason said.

"There's no hurry," Joan said. "You're both staying here tonight."

"Are we?" Jason said. "I thought –"

"It'll be a break," Elaine said.

Jason shrugged. "I'll get my jacket," he said.

They set off down the street. Philip watched Jason wheeling himself along the pavement, trying to avoid the dog shit, not looking further ahead than a few feet, relying on Philip to lead the way. It was strange. He'd thought a lot about Jason since they met that time, usually in relation to other things. Jason and booze, Jason and girls, Jason and sneering, Jason and being angry, Jason and God. Now it was just Jason and Philip.

"So what are you really doing back in Wales then?"

"The shit's hit the fan," Jason said. "They've split up."

"Yeah? When?"

"Well, it's been farting on for a while. My father got a move to Newport with the job and he didn't tell her about it for ages."

"Newport? Why didn't he tell her?"

"I don't know. He's like that sometimes. I think he just enjoys having secrets. Pathetic, really. I think she had something going with a university lecturer in Leicester anyway."

"What? Really?"

"Reading between the lines, you know." Jason grinned up at Philip. "It's good to see you again, you skinny little bastard."

They were passing the library, and the usual gang of teenagers were sitting on the wall. A short kid came up to them and tagged along.

"Yo, have you got a fag to spare?" he asked, his crew cut bobbing along to keep up with them. "C'mon, a fag, one fag, it's not a lot, like, is it?"

"How old are you?" Jason said.

"Fourteen. Next year."

"So you're thirteen then."

"Yeah. It was my birthday yesterday."

31

"Have two then." Jason took two Marlboros from his packet and handed them to the kid.

"Cheers," he said. "So where you off then?"

"Just smoke the fags." Jason said.

The kid nodded, waved and went back to the wall.

"So your mother's moving back to Cardiff, is she?" Philip asked.

"Yeah, so she says."

"And your father's in Newport?"

"Yeah."

"What about you?"

"Well, I'm here, ain't I?"

"Are they getting a divorce?"

"Probably."

"Who are you going to live with?"

"Don't know yet. Might try to get a place of my own."

Philip said nothing.

"A bungalow, obviously," Jason said.

"Somewhere around here?"

"In Wales, yeah. Down this end though Phil, not up with the sheep-shaggers."

"Cool. We can have a laugh."

"You may be right."

Jason followed Phil into the King's Arms. The bar was crowded and they had to push through. They looked pissed off when Phil elbowed through; but as soon as they saw him, Jason, in his chair, well, it was the same old shit. Breaking their necks to let him pass. Contorting like an avant-garde mime troupe. The fucking shitty cunting bastards. The vein running up his neck pulsed twice. He was so used to that vein, he could feel it now. Never used to. He decided to calm down.

Phil wriggled out from the pack at the bar with two pints, and they moved away. It was less crowded in the lounge. Jason looked around the room as he drank his pint. Most of the people here were getting on a bit. There seemed to be a birthday party going on in the corner, some old bird and her mates. There were a few middle-aged couples around the room, and one girl in her twenties with black leggings and extreme acne.

Phil's father Val, was at the front of the room. He had his red guitar strapped on, and a microphone on a stand. He seemed to have a fair amount of equipment.

"How's your father got all that stuff?" Jason asked.

"He's been saving up for years. Bought it bit by bit. Not much of it's compatible, so he spends hours in the garage, re-wiring stuff."

"What does he do again?"

"National Welsh. Buses. He's a mechanic."

Phil's father saw them, and waved. Phil gave a thumbs up, and Jason nodded.

"Now this next one is for all you cowboys," Val said. There were cheers.

"And cowgirls. Musn't forget them, am I right?"

The woman whose birthday it was shouted at Val. "Yee-ha!" Her friends cheered her.

"Ride 'em, cowboy," she added, her small, white throat tightening with the effort.

"Right, here we go then," Val said.

He strummed the intro then started singing.

"Jesus Christ!" Jason spluttered into his pint. "Who told him he could sing?"

Phil, gazing across the room, put his glass down. "That's the thing – nobody did."

The birthday party started swaying along and clapping. It seemed to be a Glen Campbell number.

"His diction leaves a lot to be desired," Jason said.

"It's like, y'know, he's the opposite of the bloke with a stutter who's word-perfect when he sings."

Val went for the chorus and Jason nearly choked.

"What did he just say? What did your father just say?" he gasped.

"He said nothing. He's singing."

"All right, what did he just sing then?"

"Well, I'm unfamiliar with this particular song, but it sounded to me like, 'I'm a nine-stone cowboy'."

Phil insisted they leave the lounge and go into the bar. Jason promised he'd try not to laugh again. Nobody noticed anyway, they were all laughing too. Phil said that Jason's laugh had a scornful quality to it that was missing from the others' laughter. It was *Under the Boardwalk* that did it, though.

"He just said 'Under the Ballcock'!" Jason shouted.

"No he fucking didn't. He said 'Under the Boardwalk', he's just not used to the microphone."

"Not used to the microphone!"

"He's too close to it. Now fucking shut up. We're going in the bar."

"I want to stay here. It's good."

"Well you can't. Come on, or I'll push you in there,"

"No you fucking won't."

"Come on then."

"All right, let me get my fags then, Jesus Christ."

It was the end of the night. Time for *The Impossible Dream*. Val's top E was a bit sharp. He adjusted it while speaking into the microphone. Like a professional.

"All right, now it's the end of the night so we'll have a nice one to finish with, and I want to hear you all singing along on this."

He played a C and began.

"To dream the impossible dream –"

He went to D for the next line, but his voice slipped under the chord. A drone, a whine. Not right. D couldn't have been right. His fingers fumbled over the strings, playing a truncated A, a mesh of F and G, a Nothing sharp minor. His eyes fled the mess and met Len's calm, ancient stare. Len had been doing entertainment for years. He knew it all. He waggled his old eyebrows and came over. A few words were exchanged, then Val nodded.

"Aye, right you are, Len. I'm with you."

"You sure?"

"Yeah, thanks."

"Sure you don't want me to do it for you?"

"No, thanks Len, thanks a lot."

"Because I could, you know."

"I know."

"Just like that."

"Yeah, I know. But I think I'll be OK now."

"Go on then," said Len, going back to his mates.

"Sorry about that, ladies and gentlemen. Here we go now."

There was sweat on his forehead, in his eyebrows. It got warm in this room. Green wallpaper and trim. Cheryl's birthday, there she was in the corner. They knew how to enjoy themselves, her crowd. They must be pushing sixty, the lot of them. Get up to all sorts. Finish this and have a pint. Concentrate now. Move back to the stool, get comfy. Cheryl over there, hell of a girl. Give her a wink. Right, here we go then.

"To Dream, the Imposs −" Val's leg twitched and jerked. His foot came down on the rhythm pedal. A jaunty bossa nova erupted all over Val's impossible dream.

"To Fight... oh Christ..."

Jason ignored the ashtray and let his fag ends drop to the scratched lino. He crushed them with his trainer, lifting his leg from the wheelchair's footrest with both hands. An odd habit, Philip thought.

"So what are you going to do?" he asked.

Jason shrugged. "About what?"

"Getting a job and all that."

"Nothing. I've got no exams."

"You could have."

"So could you."

They grinned over their pints.

"So what about money?" Philip asked.

"Benefits. Yourself?"

"The same."

"I'll get more. Disability. Mobility. Whatever."

"It's a good excuse," Philip admitted.

They grinned at each other again.

"We're the No-hope Twins," Jason said.

"Yeah," Philip laughed. "The Cripple Brothers."

35

Jason shook his head. "You're not a cripple."

"It's the same thing. What you are, I am."

"No. You'll get over it. Grow up."

Phil looked down. He was quiet. Jason gazed at his glass, then emptied it.

"Phil, hey, if you're my mate, get us a couple more and cheer up. It'll all come out in the wash."

His friend looked up again, warily.

"What will?"

"I've been through it all in my head, loads of times. It helps me sleep."

"Jason, suddenly I don't know what you're actually talking about."

He leaned forward, suddenly in Philip's face, blocking out the darts match behind him.

"You've got to go through it all in your head once before you have to do it for real. You know what I mean?"

He slipped a hip-flask out of his jacket and took a swig, then hid it away again, grinning between clenched teeth at Phil.

"I'll get the drinks like," Phil said.

"I'm thinking of having a crack at Tina Turner," Val said.

Len frowned.

"She's a woman," he said.

"Aye, but they all love a bit of Tina Turner. The youngsters love it, the couples love it, the old dears love it. *Simply the Best* – they all love that one. Singing along, dancing, everything. And see, Len, you don't have to be a woman to do that one. It's just: you're simply the best, better than all the rest, better than anyone, anyone I've ever met."

"It's better than any man, isn't it?"

"Nah," Val said. He stop wrapping up his guitar lead and frowned. "Nah, I don't think so. And anyway, it don't matter because I can just change it."

"Sex change," Len said.

They laughed.

Someone held the door open for Jason as they came through to the lounge. He wheeled through, waiting for it.

"There we are, son," the man said. "All right there? Having a good night?"

"Fuck off," Jason spat.

The man, confused, bumped into Philip as he followed Jason into the bar.

"Cheers mate," Philip said. stepping around him.

They moved across the lounge to join Val. It was twenty past eleven. Some people were putting their coats on while others were settling in. Val looked up as they approached.

"Good one," Philip said.

"Yeah, sounded great," Jason said.

"Well, aye, not bad at all, really. The Beatles medley went down well. *Travelling Light* was a lot better tonight. *Rhinestone Cowboy* was quite good. What else? Oh aye, I had a go at that one you said. That Johnny Cash one."

"*Ring of Fire*," Philip said.

"Aye, that one. All right, too."

"What about *The Impossible Dream*?"

"Yeah, bit of trouble with that one. Technical difficulties, I suppose. It's just getting used to the equipment, that's all it is. I mean, this is just my third week here, regular, because of that trouble I had."

"They don't seem to mind," Jason said, looking over at the birthday party.

"No, they're a good crowd here," Val said. "They know how to enjoy themselves. It's like a training ground see. It's all friends, we all know each other. So I can get used to the equipment and that. These people you see doing enter-tainment all around the valleys, over Bridgend way, even down in Cardiff – they all started somewhere, see."

Jason nodded twice.

"Anyway, boys, are you having a lift back? Only there's not much room in the car. For the wheelchair, like."

"Nah, it's OK," Jason said.

"Yeah, we'll walk back," Philip said.

"Do miracles, do you?"

"Your jokes are crap."

"Depends on your perspective."

"How long can you keep it up?"

"All night, if necessary."

Val coughed.

"Right well I'll see you after, boys," he said. "I'm going to have a pint here then I'll be off."

They took their time walking back and when they got in the house was dark. Burping and giggling, they slouched into the living room. Philip slumped into an armchair.

"Hey, Phil," Jason said, and Philip had to lift him out of the wheelchair and drop him on settee so he could sprawl.

"Christ, you've put on weight," Philip said, sitting down next to him.

"Muscle," Jason said, taking out his hipflask.

They watched *The Young Ones* on video, quoting favourite lines to each other. Philip didn't want any more to drink, having downed about six pints at the pub and being very thin. Jason shrugged and kept swigging whisky.

"Like your drink, don't you?" Philip said.

"Yeah, don't mind."

"And your fags."

"Uh-huh."

"What do you want to do, then?"

"What?"

"Do you want to be, like, ill?"

Jason smiled.

"No, come on," Philip said, "seriously. You're going to fuck yourself up. You're going to look crap. You won't be able to talk properly. You'll slur, and your mouth will go fat."

Jason burst out laughing.

"I never knew you cared," he said.

An hour later, Philip was falling asleep. His head kept lolling to the side, resting on Jason's shoulder.

"Come on," Jason said. "Bed. I get backache as it is. I need to get horizontal."

They took the stairs in stages, grappling in the dark.

"Hey, Phil," Jason whispered. "How come your house smells like biscuits?"

"Biscuits?" Philip had his arms around Jason's shoulders, was pulling him around the tricky turn at the top of the stairs. "What kind of biscuits?"

"Just biscuits. Ordinary ones." He sniffed. "Nice, though."

They were on the landing now. "Christ, your arms are fucking huge," Philip said, measuring his own left bicep with his right hand. The index finger and thumb almost met.

"I can make it from here," Jason said. He began crawling along on his hands, flapping his legs behind him. Philip watched him and a feeling like nausea edged into his mind. He shook it away.

"They say I shouldn't do that," Jason said as they got into Philip's room. "The physiotherapy weirdos. They say I'm twisting my spine. They're all bent, I reckon. Even the women. Perverts, you know?"

He clambered on to Philip's bed and took his trainers off. Philip went to get a quilt to put on the floor.

On the fringes of sleep, Philip heard Jason's voice. They had stopped talking a while ago, ready to rest. Now, though, his voice was soft and low. He was talking to himself.

"Fuck myself up," he was saying; then, slowly, drawing the short words out so that they were very long, "Fuck. Fuuuuuuck. Fuck. Shit. Piss."

The words, normally explosive, sounded like an oboe. Philip started to drift off.

"Phil?"

"Mmm, yeah?" He dragged the words up from somewhere.

"Do you know what my life expectancy is?"

Silence. A faint orange glow had turned the curtains into solid tubes. They looked warm.

"No."

"Nor me," Jason said.

"But it can't be bad. I mean, it's only your legs, isn't it?

"Yeah."

Silence. Shapes began to lumber around Philip's mind, huge but indefinable, alluring, hypnotic. Jason's low voice slid between them.

39

"How long have you got?" Jason asked.

Philip's reply was thick with dreams.

"I dunno, six decades, aauummmm, six years, six months, six, six, sssssixxx –"

He was asleep. Jason listened to his friend's breathing as it got deeper and slower. He breathed in mainly through his nose and out through his mouth. Breathing in took one, two, three, four seconds. Breathing out took one, two, three, four, five, six seconds and was louder. After breathing out, Phil paused for nearly one, two seconds before inhaling again. Jason always wondered if he would breathe in at all. And, after one, two seconds, just when it was getting worrying, he did.

He stopped listening, tried to sleep. He tried his technique: he was lying on his back in Treorchy, in the Rhondda Valley, in South Wales. He often like to catalogue where he was, and where the people he knew were in relation to him. If he had real trouble sleeping, he would widen the circle to include increasingly distant relatives, people he'd known at the different schools he went to but hadn't seen since.

So: Phil McKay, his new friend, was on the floor of this room. Joan and Val McKay were in the room next door. Jason's own mother, Elaine, was in the room along the landing. His father was in Newport. That concluded the immediates and he still wasn't sleepy.

In fact, although he'd been trying not to think of it, he needed a piss. He'd hoped to be asleep before it got unbearable, but no – it was fucking typical. Couldn't fucking leave him alone, not ever, not even at bed time. He got angry and that just woke him more.

"Right, well I'll go and have a fucking piss then," he muttered, pulling back the quilt.

He slid off the bed and on to the floor. In a sitting position he dragged himself backwards across the room. He passed Phil's head, knocking over a cassette case with a click.

"Sheds," Phil mumbled, then turned on his back and started snoring.

Jason reached the door. He stretched up, pulled the handle, slumped back down on his arse, then dragged himself through.

The bathroom was along the landing, it seemed, in between the spare room and Claire's room. Claire – he'd left her out of his list. Hadn't even thought of her. He hadn't seen her since he got to the McKay's house. Perhaps her name would have been the one, made him dozy, put him to sleep. Then he wouldn't be dragging his arse along the landing in the middle of the fucking night.

He reached up, opened the door, slid into the bathroom, closed the door and turned his head. His heart missed a beat then came down hard on the next. There was someone there. A figure stood in the darkness of the silent shithouse, not a very tall figure, in fact.

"You told me you don't go upstairs," the figure whispered.

Squinting, Jason saw a glow. It was green, or yellow, perhaps blue. Very faint, it shimmered somewhere up ahead. Next to it, carrying a trace of it, was the silhouette of Claire McKay in tartan pyjamas. He pulled the front of his t-shirt over his boxer shorts.

"I didn't know anyone was in here," he whispered.

Claire was silent.

"Sorry," Jason added.

"OK."

"Shall I turn the light on?"

"No. Come and see this." He crawled over to her. She was standing by the hand basin, looking into it. The glow was coming from there. He craned his neck but couldn't see. He was too low.

"Come up higher," Claire said.

"I can't, can I?"

"Sit on the toilet seat and lean over."

Her voice was very precise, just as he remembered it. He clambered up, knocking over the toilet brush.

"I've knocked over your toilet brush," he whispered.

"OK," she said. "Lean over. Can you see them now?"

He leaned his elbows on the basin and looked into the water. He couldn't think of anything to say. Claire leaned her own elbows on the basin and looked into the water. Then she looked over at Jason.

"What do you think?"

"What are they meant to be?"

"They're my universe fish."

They were plastic fish, about eight of them, in assorted colours. They were weighted in such a way that they didn't sink to the bottom of the water but hung and bobbed just under the surface. At the bottom of the basin lay a small torch in rubber casing with a green filter over the bulb. The multi-coloured fish drifted over the torch in twos or threes, glowing faintly as they did. Jason and Claire leaned on the side and looked in, and the undulating glow rippled over their faces.

"What are you doing?" Jason said.

"Watching my universe fish," Claire said. "Do you think I'm immature?"

"I don't know you well enough to say. How old are you?"

"Thirteen."

"Probably not then."

"Doesn't it look good, though? The universe fish?"

"It looks like some plastic fish and a torch in a sink," Jason said, shrugging his big shoulders.

He watched her copy the gesture with her small shoulders.

"I'll switch the torch off then," she said.

She rolled up her pyjama sleeve, reached into the water and the torch clicked off. It was suddenly very dark. Jason breathed out, and heard Claire breathe in. Then he realised he could still see the fish. They were still glowing, but even more faintly now, just smudges of green.

"Yeah," Jason said, "that's impressive."

"Fluorescent paint." Claire's voice was pleased.

They leaned on the basin in silence. Their heads moved slightly closer to the glow, as if it were a fire. The dark gathered at their backs, like someone wrapping a quilt around them and drawing it together.

"Why do you do this?" Jason whispered.

"It looks good," Claire whispered back across the water. "I love things that look like this."

"Why do you call them universe fish?"

"I made it up when I was little. They were supposed to swim through the universes."

Jason snorted.

"What's the matter?" Claire asked.

"You." Jason tried to grin. "What are you on?"

Claire raised her eyebrows at him. Her eyes were narrow, green, calm.

"Don't you ever do things like this?" she asked.

"I'm a bit old, really."

"Am I?"

Jason looked at the universe fish, then slowly up at Claire. He could just make out her hair, tied in a ponytail that curled around her neck and trailed down the front of her pyjamas.

"Not yet," he said.

"Good." She smiled. "Do you like toasted sandwiches?"

"What?"

Jason wondered what time it was. It had to be around two.

"Yeah, I don't mind them."

"Do you want one? Now, I mean."

"What, are you hungry then? At this time of night?"

She reached into the water and pulled out the plug. The fish started swirling round and round.

"I always have a toasted sandwich on Friday night," Claire said.

Would she leave soon? He really needed a piss now. The sound of the water wasn't helping. Claire took the fish out, shook them and put them away in a Pot Noodle container. The glow faded.

"Can you go downstairs on your own?"

"Can you?"

"Shall I make a sandwich for you then?"

"Why not?"

She left without another word, taking the universe fish with her. He got down from the toilet, dragged his body across the floor, locked the bathroom door, and crawled back to the toilet. Then he sat down to piss. He heard her moving around in her room, then going downstairs, Turning his head to the ceiling, he launched a weary, knowing look upwards, but he wasn't really weary and he didn't feel knowing.

Crawling along the landing, he could see a faint light from the kitchen, could feel the soft carpet tickling his legs as he moved. He could hear a car, streets away, going too fast. He headed for the stairs and heard Philip mumbling in his sleep. He pushed the bedroom door closed on his way past.

4. MARCH 1992

Still no niche. Philip could have drawn a map of all the quiet places in the valley where you could sit in a daze, feeling like a stray molecule in an amazingly complex circulatory system, as you watched the cars slowly drag themselves up Penrhys hill before hitting the big dipper drop, flashing past the cemetery and down into Tylorstown at sixty, all under a bowl of damp, bubbly clouds; but there had to be more to life, as they said. Besides, the dole were hassling him to get a job.

So he went to a temping agency in Cardiff, did a laughable aptitude test, then went for a drink with Jason. Three weeks later, Philip was a filing clerk at an insurance firm in the city centre.

The job was OK. Peaceful. Between slotting dusty, buff-coloured folders into grey steel cabinets, he meditated, gazing out at the city streets. The mornings were the worst because then he had to file the current folders which were kept in the main office, and people always wanted them right now. But in the afternoons he usually went upstairs to the attic to file the cleared cases.

The attic was the name given to a series of hallways at the top of the building, each seemingly superimposed on the other, with an odd corridor running around them at varying heights. There were oddly positioned windows at unexpected angles, giving unusual views. It was like being in an Escher drawing, Philip thought.

It was silent in the attic, apart from the hiss of air-conditioning. Philip would find some hidden corner and watch the street scenes or the dust on the window ledge. It wasn't what you'd call a niche but, once again, he'd found a bolt-hole.

"Philip?"

A door opened somewhere in the attic. He was gazing at a web on the window frame strung with dead flies. Through its mesh, he could see the red neon sign in the Capitol Centre. He jumped up at the voice.

"Yeah?"

Terry appeared from an oblique angle.

"You're doing the cleared filing, are you?" he asked.

"Yeah." Philip nodded.

"Well, we're looking for a file. The client's been on the phone a couple of times and we can't find her details."

"What's the reference?"

"FNG Blue 49186220, surname Rees."

"Right, I'll look for it."

They trooped out of the attic and down to the office.

"OK, so check the cabinets in case it's been filed wrongly," Terry said, "check the filing to be done, and check Richard's desk."

Terry grinned and Philip did the same. Richard was the joke member of staff. Philip felt sorry for Richard, though, who was still recovering from his wife's suicide and his own subsequent nervous breakdown. His odd behaviour was common currency.

From 2.30 to 3.15 Philip looked through the office for the file. He checked the cabinets, making sure the name Rees hadn't been put in the Rhys section or in the Reeves section or in the small, exotic Preese section. It wasn't. Then he checked to see if the FNG file had been put in the FMG section or the ENG section. It hadn't. So he checked all the Blue 491 files in case it was there but in the wrong numerical position. It wasn't. Finally he checked around the absent Richard's desk, coming across a picture of Norman Tebbit with the eyes burnt out and a metal cough sweet tin containing a dead insect, but not the missing file.

He went for a rest in the stair-well, and slumped on the bannister. His head was pounding and his eyes were fucked. He desperately wanted to lie in a dark room listening to the Cocteau Twins. Soon they would be on to him, wanting to know where that file was. Through the window, across the road, a banner hung from Queen Street Station, shouting at him: NEXT TIME TAKE THE TRAIN. Every time he caught sight of the sign he whispered, "I took the fucking train this time. And I'll take the fucking train next time. So fucking shut up about it." There were variations in this as time wore on, eventually reducing the statement to "Fuck off."

So much for his bolt-hole. It wasn't so much the work, which he could ignore. It was the effort of being pleasant to people all day. When he got home he was too tired to talk. Everyone patted Philip's back for sticking at it. But he couldn't see how doing this was morally superior to doing any other thing, or to not doing anything at all.

Back in the office he knelt in the shelves, pretending to look for the file, though he'd actually given up. He flipped through a couple of file tags and there, in between FNG Green 77658101 and FNG Green 77658102 was the file. Someone had stuck a Blue file in with the Green ones. It wasn't in numerical or alphabetical order; fuck, it wasn't even the right colour. Someone – Philip basically – had just stuffed it in between some others, completely at random, so he could go up to the attic and sit on a windowsill.

They were closing in, he could smell their aftershave. He spent three seconds crouched at the shelf, holding the file, thinking, then grabbed it and moved through the office to Richard's desk.

He was at the dentist's that afternoon so Philip stuck the file in a stupid, confused position behind his VDU. Then, stepping back, he started looking for it again.

Eight seconds later Terry arrived, with Dave and Steve. They came to a stop, opened their mouths to speak, and then Philip found the file. He plucked it, with obvious difficulty, and a certain amount of disbelief, from behind the VDU. He scrutinised the tag. Then he turned and faced the audience.

"FNG Blue 49186220, surname Rees?"

Terry, Dave and Steve blinked.

"Behind Richard's screen," Philip said, holding the file out.

They took it and turned it over in their hands, their six eyes slowly swivelling. Philip raised his eyebrows and started to walk.

"Right, I'll get on with the cleared filing then," he said.

"That's where you found it?" Terry asked.

"Yeah, I'd looked for it everywhere else, then I just saw the tag sticking out."

He joined the office's main artery and made for the door.

"Well done Philip, thanks for that," Dave said.

"OK," Philip said, and left.

Up the stairs he went, grinning, and ambled into the attic. Down to the big city from the sheep-shagging valleys, and he'd beaten the bastards. He wondered how Jason would have dealt with that. He didn't know but he was sure it would involve a fair amount of swearing. Philip wandered through the attic, glancing at dust. Jason would have given them shit, told them just how big a part the missing file played in his mental landscape. Which was true and honest, of course, but it would have lost him the job.

He came to the window he liked, and looked out across the car park. Sharp suited men and women scurried around, dodging between cars, clutching briefcases and folders, laughing and frowning at the same time.

Richard was probably the only person in the office who didn't deserve what Philip had just done to him. He frowned – there was a moral to this story, some universal truth oozing out. All he could say for sure was that there would be more of this. That this, in fact, would become the fabric of his life, that this would be Philip McKay, this and nothing else. Over at the station, the sign shouted at him again: NEXT TIME TAKE THE TRAIN.

"I fucking will," Philip called to it; and he fucking did.

Jason came up for a visit at Easter. His mother was living in Cardiff, the divorce in progress. He didn't have much to say about it, except that sharing a house with his mother, auntie and gran was a nightmare. All his clothes smelt of pot pourri. They went to the Windsor Hotel for a drink and to check out the entertainment. In the dingy room with the sloping floor and burgundy carpet, they sat watching Mike Starr, who sang Righteous Brothers songs to backing tapes and fiddled with his genitals.

"When I was a kid," he said, "a mountain bike was a girl from Aberdare."

There was laughter, and a shout from the corner.

"Anyone here from Aberdare?"

A gang of exuberantly pissed-up girls pointed to their friend, a blonde with a low cut top.

Mike leered at the tits and said, "Nice to see you both."

His hands fled to his crotch for a quick grope.

"It must be a nervous thing," Philip said.

Jason scowled. He was sober, and not keen on it. He was thinking, thinking all the time, that's what he did – think. And the problem, he thought, was one of irony. Phil could sit there, like he was now, with his chin on his hand and his legs crossed, signalling detachment. His body language said he was taking the piss. But people would assume, looking at Jason in a wheelchair, that this was the best he could do. To be someone with as obviously limited life as the cripple, a night out like this must be *nice*. Perhaps it was even *lovely*.

Jason watched Phil laugh when Mike Starr told a joke. It was so obvious that he wasn't laughing at the joke, but at the laughter. Any fucker could see that. But if Jason laughed, or even smiled, kind of wryly amused, or laconic or whatever, everybody would think he liked this shit. A handicapped bloke enjoying a proper night out. Fuck it – another angle. The bastards were making sure there was nothing Jason could do, nowhere he could go, no options for him.

"What's the matter with you?" Phil asked.

"This is crap," Jason said. "Isn't there anywhere better?"

"Not really. It's all about the same around here. It's quite funny though, in a way."

"Ha fucking ha."

Phil could be subtle about it, but not Jason. To make sure they knew, he had to hammer the message home. Fine then, that's what he had to do. He changed gear, drank and smoked more and more, sneered harder and harder, did it straight into people's eyes.

Philip looked over at Jason, who seemed to be angry about something.

"Do you want to go, then?"

Jason knocked back the rest of his pint.

"Nah, not yet. Get 'em in."

In front of Philip at the bar was a corduroy shirt. Its wearer turned his head to talk to someone, and Philip saw the flat, no-nonsense frown of Minty. Michael Minton was the sort of boy who'd pin you up against the bottle bank and headbutt you. If you were a girl he'd fuck you. As far as Philip could see, there were always boys stepping forward to be butted, and girls stepping forward to be fucked. The good old bottle bank in the library car park would rock and clank in its rusty puddle.

Philip came out with a bunch of books one day, and started crossing the car park. He was going to walk home along the railway line. As he got closer to the car park's edge, where the recycling skips were, he saw Minty's car. He had an Astra hatchback in those days and it was parked at an anti-social angle, like it had skidded to a stop almost jammed between the two metal boxes – the bottle bank and the can bank.

Philip got closer, trying to think himself invisible, but not able to stop looking. Minty, spectated by dribbling friends, was kicking the shit out of someone. On either side, the metal boxes penned them in. Minty's car was the front door of this cosy play house. The victim's only escape was out the back way, across the dog-shitty grass and up onto the railway.

Philip could, of course, have gone home a different way. Instead, he circled Minty's metal boxing ring, carefully and quietly, watching. He squatted in some bushes, just across the river, his ankles aching as they kept him clinging to the steep slope. One hand was fastened to some roots to stop him sliding, the other held on to his library books.

He watched Minty laying into the poor bastard, heard the clang of his head against the hollow bank, saw his expensive trainers drag through the rusty water, and he thought the bloke had had enough. Minty kept stopping, stepping back, then starting again, like an artist trying to judge when his work is finished. And Philip, now in aching, sliding, clutching agony, watched; waiting to see how it would end, what goes on in these situations.

Minty stopped. Stepped back. Looked down at his victim, slumped on the ground. Stood silent among his giggling mates, and narrowed his eyes. Philip's eyes narrowed too, trying to see what Minty saw. How did he judge when enough was enough? Philip would have stopped ages ago.

Still silent, Minty turned and slid back into his car. The others followed, jeering at the bloke on the floor. The Astra screeched out and away. Philip stayed for the end, the anticlimax, where the victim rolled himself upright, sat against the bottle bank for a while, touching his face, then picked up his scattered belongings, his fags and lighter, keys and wallet, then limped off.

Now here he was, Minty, with friends and admirers queuing up to have a few words with him, his latest bird spot-welded to him by the thigh. Philip was standing right behind him at the bar, watching his bird slide her hand into the tight arsepocket of his jeans. Minty was talking, serious as always, to a mate, obviously discussing important matters, ignoring the female rucksack strapped to his side, like men should.

And right then Philip's grin popped up. He'd had it for a while now. He'd find himself watching something not a bit funny, when his brain would register humour. The grin would then slide out into the world, out into people's eyes. He always tried to hide it, in case someone asked what the fuck he was grinning at, and he wouldn't know, so he wouldn't be able to tell them, so they'd smash his face in with a brick.

But Minty's bird turned, right then, before he could wipe it away, and looked at him funny. Some skinny, scruffy little nothing was grinning at her. Better still, grinning at her boyfriend, the one and only Minty. Philip did his panicky best to look indifferent, got the drinks, and hurried back to the table. Perhaps it was time to leave. Yeah, they'd have this last one, looking as inoffensive as little kittens, and stroll out. A poor disabled boy and his kind-hearted friend having a nice night out. He settled down to look normal.

"Why don't you join in the conversation, love? You been fucking staring at us all night."

It was a girl on the next table, and she was talking to Jason.

"Nah, I'd rather just watch, thanks," Jason said.

"What's so fascinating you can't mind your own business?"

Jason looked thoughtful. "Ever been to a zoo?"

Philip grabbed his arm.

"For fuck's sake, Jason."

"What?"

"Cut it out."

The girls on the next table were chattering to each other; high-pitched, indignant, loud.

"Drink up," Philip said, "we're off."

"Why?"

"We just are."

"But I'm just starting to enjoy myself."

"Oh God."

Mike Starr started singing *Relax*, thrusting his balls at a camp looking man who sniggered into his gin and tonic.

"Smash the system, yeah?" Jason drawled, raising a fist at Mike Starr.

Philip ignored him, sat looking straight ahead. He knew that every time someone cast a glance in Jason's direction, as people will, Jason was sneering at them. He bolted his pint down.

"Ready then?"

He turned to Jason and saw that his glass was full of whiskey again. He looked from the glass into Jason's eyes, dumbstruck by this miracle. Jason grinned, and tapped himself on the chest, just where his heart would be; there was a muffled tink-tink-tink.

"Oh, for fuck's sake –" Philip groaned.

"Fancy a top up, old chap?" Jason slurred.

He refused to budge, just kept refilling his glass from the hip-flask. He was now laughing out loud at the singer's catarrh-clogged croon, at the people dancing. Philip kept glancing over at Minty, but trying not to make eye-contact.

"Nice leggings, love. Hey, he did it again!" Jason shouted.

Philip gritted his teeth.

"He just felt his balls! Again!"

Now even Mike Starr was watching.

"Why do you think he does that. Phil? Phil?"

"Have you got a problem?"

The man who collected the glasses was standing over them in his rugby shirt.

"Pardon?" Jason said.

"Have you got a problem, son?"

Jason looked at his wheelchair and patted his legs.

"Well, dad," he said, "yes I have, actually. I didn't know it was that obvious, but well done you for spotting it. Cheers!"

He waved his glass in the man's face, then knocked it back.

"Best you both leave now."

"What? But I'm a paying customer."

"No he's not." The girls on the next table joined in. "He's got his own, it's in his pocket."

Jason pulled out the hip-flask.

"It's not my own, it's my dad's," he said.

"Yeah OK, mate, we're just on our way." Philip started putting his jacket on, "Sorry about all this, like."

"Your friend's had a few too many, that's all. Happens all the time."

"Yeah," Philip nodded. "I'll take him home, it'll be all right."

Jason was having trouble getting out from the tables and chairs.

"Give him some coffee and get him to bed," the man said. "That's your best bet."

"Yeah, right, I'll do that."

"You OK there mate?" the man said.

Jason grunted, his chair stuck. The man moved over to help him, grabbed the handles of the chair.

"Get your fucking hands off me."

It wasn't a shout, but it was loud. Everyone was looking. Minty was looking. The man tried to laugh it off.

"Easy there, mate. I wasn't even touching you."

"It's OK, really." Philip was rushing around the table to Jason. "No problem, we'll be gone in a minute."

The man nodded, put his hands on the chair again.

"Don't fucking touch me!"

"Calm down, son, I'm not touching you." The man was trying hard not to make a scene. "I'm just trying to give you a hand with the old chariot here."

"That's the magic word, you MOTHERFUCKER!" Jason screamed.

Everyone froze for a few seconds, and Philip ran around the chair, got in front of the glass man and pushed Jason out from the table. They accelerated across the room, crushing toes and spilling drinks. Jason was saying something, jeering, but Philip wasn't listening. Minty's corduroy shirt and matching girlfriend went by in a blur, and they were out. Philip kept pushing, and they were speeding down Cardiff Street.

"Are we going on somewhere else?" Jason's voice was bright.

"You twat," Philip said. He was breathing hard. "You silly, stupid, fucked up bastard. You prick. I mean, Christ. You arsehole. You fucking mindless cunt. You don't know anything. Fuck all. You're so fucking thick. Jesus."

"Yeah, well fuck you," Jason said. "What the fuck do you know?"

"More than you."

"Yeah? Like what?"

"I know what a stupid bastard you are for a start."

"You don't know fuck all. You're the prick."

"What, did you reckon that was clever or something? Think it fucking proved something, did you? All it proved was what a prick you are. At least I know how to fucking survive, don't I?"

"Yeah? Well, fucking good luck to you." Jason turned around in the chair as they hurtled along. "Be nice to them and they'll be nice to you," he said. "OK, go and fucking do it then. Go apologise, you daft cunt, stop pushing me around and go back there." He stuck his finger up, almost poking Philip in the mouth. "This is your life Phil – go and fucking live it. Just don't come complaining to me," he put on a mocking, whiny voice, "because they don't understand you, oh, you've got nothing in common with them and, oh poor me, there's no one around here I can discuss Dostoy-bastard-evsky with, what can I do? Nobody around here understands me, I'm soooo aloooooone." He snapped off the whiny voice. "Don't come complaining to me, and don't tell me I don't fucking know anything."

By this time they'd come to the end of the street. The wheelchair bumped off the kerb and into the gutter. Jason nearly fell out.

"And watch where you're going," he growled.

Phil smirked.

They went home and talked shit until gone three.

On Easter Sunday morning, Jason woke from a dream in which his wheelchair started talking to him. He couldn't remember what it had said, but it seemed sad about something. Then its wheels started to melt, very slowly turning to jelly.

He shook his head and joined Phil's family downstairs. They were in a good, Bank Holiday mood. Claire, barefoot in jeans and a T-shirt, was curled up on the settee with a Smarties egg. Val was in good form, making silly jokes about everything anyone said, his greying quiff immaculate. And Joan fussed around, happy to be a housewife for a day or two. He sat with them in the living room, unshaven, his head fuzzy. His wheelchair seemed wrong, too big and ugly to be stuck in the middle of their room. It made tracks in the carpet.

Yawning and scratching his head, Phil turned on the television, then slumped into an armchair. There was a discussion on about Jesus. They were debating the importance of miracles to Christianity.

"Phil, nobody's watching that," Joan said.

"I like a bit of background noise," Phil said.

"You want background noise?" Val asked.

"Well, yeah, I do."

"Oh, I'll give you some background noise," Val said, smiling. He winked at Jason.

"No, not that," Phil groaned.

"You don't know what I'm going to say," Val protested.

"I think we do, Dad," Claire said.

"Can you believe this?" Val said to Jason, who smiled a bit, still feeling weird.

Joan came back through from the kitchen. She pointed at the television, looking at Philip.

"Yeah, but –" Phil said.

"He likes a bit of background noise," Claire said.

"I said I'll give him some background noise," Val said.

"Oh, not now, Val," Joan said. "Save it until tonight. Give us a bit of peace."

"What do you think, Phil?" Val asked.

"I just said I like a bit of noise in the background, that's all."

Val nudged Jason's arm.

"See, that's how I get them to behave," he said.

Jason felt faint. If Val didn't spit out the punchline before long, he might vomit. Was he expected to keep a smile on his face the whole time? But he did keep it, because Val was a nice bloke. They were a nice family. He felt so fragile this morning.

"I threaten them with the guitar," Val said, grinning at him.

Jason laughed, sounding like a steam valve releasing pressure. He caught Claire's glance, her raised eyebrows, before she went back to her Smarties.

It went a bit quiet then, apart from the television. Jason listened to the discussion. A man said that the miracles in the New Testament were an interesting part of the story, but not to be taken literally. Another man disagreed.

"I've been to a healing," he said.

Jason felt his lip starting to curl. Religious people – it was automatic.

"I've seen a woman who had no use of her legs, and I saw her being actually healed. She still writes to me. Every morning she runs around the lake in front of her home. She's just so glad to be alive."

Jason swallowed hard.

"But the point is, it is vital to Christianity that we accept the literal truth of Christ's resurrection. He was God, as well as man: that is what separates Christianity from a sort of vague humanism."

Jason's sneer didn't form. His lip twitched. He thought about it – just getting up one morning, coming downstairs to your family, just like this. It had never occurred to him before, not as simple as that. In all this bullshit, could it really be? Was there someone, somewhere, running around some lake? Just like that, your slate wiped clean, start again, year zero. His mind would stay the same, just the body changed. Without the chair, he'd be unbeatable.

The simple things, though, they were the real bastards in this. You could enjoy a nice long fantasy of getting dressed for a night out, walking into a bar, flirting and being sexy with your cynicism, But when you imagined, really imagined, in detail, putting your jeans on, and your shoes, and walking out through your front door; when you imagined it, when someone on telly said it's happened, some woman somewhere just waking up one morning, just like today; when you imagined it, when it hit you, when you first got the full picture, felt it like it was, like you were feeling it now, in the McKays' living room, when you felt it –

Claire looked over at Jason. That vein in his neck was throbbing, the thick blue one that ran up to his square jaw. His forehead was all wrinkled up, and he looked confused. Claire had seen all this before, in the nights, when they ate toasted sandwiches together in the kitchen while everyone else slept. When he talked to her he snarled and whined and swore, and she said stupid things to him in silly voices, and then he laughed at her.

She wanted to touch his hand. Phil and her father were in the room as well though. It wasn't just her and Jason. She wanted him to snap out of it. He was having one of his wide-awake nightmares.

Joan came in with a Tesco bag.

"I suppose you're a bit old for this, but here you are anyway," she said, handing Philip an Easter egg. "We all like a bit of chocolate, don't we?"

"Aye, too much, some of us," Val said, patting his paunch. "No worry about that with you, though," he said to Philip. "You remind me of this lurcher I used to have. She'd go through three tins of dog food a day. Didn't put a pound on."

"She was probably an ectomorph," Phil said.

"No, she was definitely a lurcher," Val chuckled.

Joan approached Jason, shyly. He was a big lad. Imposing.

"Do you like chocolate as much as this lot?" she smiled.

Jason looked up at her. She was blurry. He nodded.

"There we are, that's from all of us. I know you're a bit old, but I still buy Val an egg every year," she said.

"Aye, and sometimes it's a chocolate one," Val said.

Jason took the Mars egg from Joan, and put it on his lap.

His hands were shaking as he looked at it and he had no words for the family. The gold wrapping shimmered before his eyes.

Claire jumped up from the settee and bounced across to the television, going, "La la la la la la!"

"Let's see what's on the other side," she said, and changed channels.

"Oh no, not the bloody Waltons," Philip groaned.

Claire giggled loudly, standing right in front of Jason, shielding him from view.

"Hey, there's nothing wrong with the Waltons," said Val. "You can learn a lot from the Waltons."

"Listen to him," Joan said, and disappeared, back to the kitchen.

"I think the Waltons are based on a real family," Val said. "I read that somewhere."

"No, you're thinking of the Swiss Family Robinson," Phil said.

"Were they the ones with Grizzly Adams in?"

"Grizzly Adams? No."

"What was he then?"

"He was just him. He was an entirely separate entity."

"Was he? Poor bugger," Val said.

Claire smiled and walked back to the settee, past Jason, who looked up at her. He couldn't see her properly. He wiped his left eye, and he could make out her expression, just a flash before she wiped it off. She was smiling, and she nodded twice. Then she went back to the settee, to her remote control and her Smarties egg.

5. May 1992.

After two months in the office Philip had taken up smoking. It gave him some way to divide the tedium into defined slices of time, which began and ended with an endorphin-rush.

He has also started counting the number of words he spoke each day. He subtracted all the ones he said automatically, or didn't mean, or which failed to interest him even as they were coming out of his mouth, and this gave him the seasonally adjusted figure. It was tricky, but it kept his mind occupied.

"Good morning (nil). Morning (nil). Good weekend? (nil) Oh not bad (nil). I'll make a list of the recent correspondence cases, then (nil). The cumulative on-hand total is 64 for the week ending the twenty-second (nil). Nah, I thought I'd pop over to Burger King. Thanks anyway (nil). Yeah, it does get a bit boring (4). Yeah, I'll pop in one night, sounds like a laugh (nil). Goodnight (1)."

He didn't see much of Jason, who was still unemployed and living in Cardiff. Philip spent his weekends in bed, reading all the new books he was buying with his wages. He couldn't face talking to people, fell out of the habit, even with Jason. Then, one Friday, Philip got stuck in a party, and his bolt-hole fell in, trapping him.

It was Sue's thirtieth birthday. She wasn't very high in the office hierarchy, but she was very popular so everyone had the afternoon off.

"We're diverting the calls at the switchboard," Terry had told him.

Philip beamed. He was already walking down Queen Street, already smoking in a cafe with a French novel, making eyes at the girl on the next table.

"The party starts at one," Terry said.

"Ah, well, I don't know if I can make it," Philip said, as usual.

Terry just laughed and said, "You won't have any choice, mate. You'll have to make it. It's in the office."

Philip's skin started crawling.

"The party's in the office?" he said.

"Yeah, but it's OK," Terry said. "It'll be a laugh, we've got a load of drink in. It's just so we can all clock off at five as usual and no-one will know we've been on the piss."

He avoided, he avoided, he scurried around, went up and down in the lift, hid in the bogs, muttering, "The horror, the horror," tried to cheer himself up by laughing at that, heard someone singing a Bon Jovi song, heard a conversation at the pissers about whether their boss took it up the arse, heard the assertion that she would, tonight, in just a few hours time, heard the laughter of the dead, the cheery back-slapping, back-stabbing banter, felt very, very old.

He heard countless ways to cheat on income tax, to get expensive cars, to improve the performance of various football teams. He heard jokes, jokes about shagging, about AIDS, about gay vicars, gay zoo keepers, lesbian nuns, nympho-maniac nuns, car thieves, Scousers, sheep-shaggers, Pakis, spastics, epileptics, Downs Syndrome babies and about nothing really but with lots of puns.

At a quarter to five, the male staff gave Sue an enormous comedy penis as a present, and, to everyone's delight and wonder, she gave it a frighteningly realistic blow-job, ending by biting off the tip. Philip went to get his coat. He had a clanging headache. The tinny, trebly Bananarama rattling from the tin speakers of a cheap tape deck didn't help. He lurked in the toilets, waiting for his watch to beep.

At three minutes to five he made his way through the corridors to the lift. He went through a set of double doors and saw Sue. She was on her knees, retching and puking. There was drool on her blouse. She looked up at Philip through the tears in her eyes, and said, "I think I've swallowed a bit of it."

Before the train had left the suburbs, Philip was asleep. The anonymity of the train's upholstery always relaxed him. Dreaming of mahogany staircases and clown-faced guitarists, he was carried back up into the valley.

He got in and sat in front of *Wales Today* with a plate of

chicken nuggets. Claire was buzzing around, getting ready to go out.

"Where are you off tonight?" Philip asked.

"Rehearsals," Claire said, slipping on her Reeboks.

"For what?"

"School play."

"Oh yeah? What are you doing?"

"*Look Back in Anger.*"

"What? You're fourteen, for God's sake."

Claire smiled at Philip's face.

"Is that a problem?" she asked.

"Well, yeah, I'd have thought so. Don't you think it's a bit advanced for your age-group?"

Claire leaned over Philip and tapped his forehead.

"It's all in the mind," she said.

"Well look, I've got a book of Derek Jarman scripts upstairs – why don't you take that in tomorrow? The first formers could do *Jubilee* for the PTA."

"Three points: first, it's Saturday tomorrow. Second: I believe Mr Hayhurst prefers *Sebastiane*. Third: it's actually the Upper Sixth that are doing the play, but Mr Hayhurst asked if I'd be Alison."

"Bloody weirdo."

"It's my talent, Phil, simple as that."

"Who's playing Jimmy, for God's sake?"

"Ben Wilmott."

"Oh, that's all right then."

"Why?"

"Well, he's bent, isn't he?"

"Is he?"

"I'd have thought so."

Claire grimaced and threw something at him. An envelope.

"Well I'm a prole, ain't I?" Philip said. "You can't expect anything else from me. I tell you, if I was a pop star, every-one'd lap it up. Authentic, they'd say." He looked at the letter. "What's this?"

"Work it out for yourself," Claire said, "prole," and went to get her coat.

The envelope had a Newport postmark, and the instruction, "Pass on your postcode – you're not properly addressed without it." It was addressed to him, but his postcode was missing. He didn't recognise the handwriting, and he didn't know anybody in Newport. His dinner tray was still on his lap. His laces were undone but he hadn't taken his shoes off. He couldn't work out who the letter was from. But he could remember the TV jingle to which the postcode message formed the lyrics: a chirpy, optimistic tune to contain fifteen syllables of advice from the Post Office.

Claire popped her head around the door, said, "That's right, it's a letter," and left.

Philip opened the envelope:

Phil,

It's Jason. I'm staying at my father's place at the moment. I don't know why, it just seemed a good idea at the time. I wanted a change of scene. My parents are getting divorced RIGHT AT THIS VERY MOMENT. Even as we speak, hordes of pricey solicitors are taking it all apart, and putting it into two mounds. I just wish I was five years younger, then I could watch them fight over who doesn't get custody.

Actually, that's basically why I'm in Newport. We were all staying at my grandmother's house in Cardiff – me, my mother and my auntie Ellen, who still lives at home for some reason. It's weird, actually. The house is in Llanishen, which is about three miles from the city centre. Anyway, it's a quiet little suburb, full of trees and wide pavements. All the buildings are low and tasteful. You know the type of thing, like in 'The Good Life'. Anyway, in the middle of all this niceness there's this FUCKING HUMUNGOUS LUMP of a building, just a big grey slab, really huge. It would probably take half an hour just to walk around it, and it's about sixteen storeys high. It looks like it's come bursting out of the ground, like in that film (you know the one I mean). It's an Inland Revenue building, and Ellen works there. We're just across the road from it. It's so big and close that in the afternoon it casts a shadow across us. So every day Ellen gets up, gets dressed, eats her Bran Flakes, and walks along the street, across the road, and into this building. Then she "pops in" for lunch, goes back, and comes home again at six.

So we were all in this house, with this fucking SLAB looming over us all the time, and I was just getting on everybody's tits (and that's three pairs, or six individual tits we're talking about). There was my mother on the phone all the time doing legal stuff, and my grandmother doing some kind of running commentary on the STATE OF THE WORLD TODAY, and how her only criticism of Mrs Thatcher was that she "didn't go far enough", and Ellen toddling back and fore all the time, depressing the piss out of me.

So anyway, everyone got irritated with me, even Ellen who usually doesn't talk when she gets home from work, so now I'm in Newport. My father's living in this flat which is pretty swish, a bachelor pad sort of thing, like you see in 70's porn films. He's out all day at work, and I'm sitting here bored out of my mind. I've been doing a bit of meditation, like you said, but it only really works when I've had a few. Luckily, Papa's usually well-stocked. If not, I take a ride down to the liquor store, which is Spar, basically, and get some supplies in. I'm building up quite a rapport with the bloke who serves there. He goes, "What's your poison today then?" and I tell him, and he goes, "Starting early?" and I say, "No, finishing late."

So, that's me sorted.

There's a lot of shit happening with the Social Services and all these other people right now, trying to ensure that my life becomes wonderful, but I think I've given them the slip for the time being. With any luck I'll be getting my own place in Cardiff before long.

There's this guy I've got to ring about a flat in Llandaff or somewhere.

Anyway, how are things with you? Have you got a job yet? Have you been beaten up yet? Is your old man still doing entertainment? And if so, has he extended his patch beyond just that one pub? And how's your sister?

Look Phil, I'm really incredibly bored. Want to come up? Or I could come down. Whatever. Write to me and we'll sort something out. Unless, of course, a cripple doesn't fit in with your current lifestyle, in which case fuck off, eat shit and die. Cheers, Phil, see you, Jason.

Philip put the letter on the tray. Val came in with a cup of coffee, followed by Joan.

They sat down, sighed, and kicked off their shoes. Val picked up the paper, Joan started leafing through *Best* magazine. *Wales Today* finished and *Watchdog* started.

"Her face is lop-sided as hell," Val said.

"I think she's quite pretty," Joan said.

"Well, I wouldn't go that far," Val said. "She's got what you'd call a characterful face, really, it expresses a lot."

"What does it express, Val?"

"Not just one thing. Many things. She's a complicated woman. Like all of us."

"So you're a complicated woman, are you?" Joan said.

Philip got up and carried his tray out to the kitchen, then had a piss while looking at himself in the mirror. He was wearing a shirt and tie, and had a side-parting. He was starting to get bags under his eyes. As yet, they weren't contoured, just patches of darkness. He sighed, coughed, then nodded once at his reflection. He went up to his room and rummaged through his tapes. He plucked Bowie's *Aladdin Sane* from between some Smiths bootlegs and fast-forwarded to the title track. Then he got his skinny black jeans out of the wardrobe and slashed some lines in them with his craft knife. He slid the volume up and got his suede boots from under the bed, and a white T-shirt. Bowie crooned away as Philip got a black marker and wrote on the T-shirt, "The air is full of our screams, but habit is a great deadner". He pulled his clothes on and went downstairs to the bathroom mirror. His hair was still neatly parted, so he got a tube of wet-look gel and messed it up. His hair got darker, from brown to black, but there was still something missing. He got a small band-aid from the cupboard and stuck it on his forehead, next to his eyebrow. He pulled on his jacket, stuck his notepad and pen in his pocket and went into the living room.

"Right, I'm off to see Jason," he said.

As Claire walked to the school for the rehearsal it got suddenly dark. Looking back, she saw that the sun had sunk behind the mountain. Clusters of grey cloud had closed in, damping down the last light, dirtying the horizon like coffee-scum.

She passed a hundred houses on her way. Caught out by the sun's abrupt descent their curtains were still open, their lights not yet turned on. Claire glanced into the living rooms; blue and orange grottoes lit by TV and coal-effect fires. Indistinct people merged with the furniture they sat in, fabric to fabric, loathe to move. All down the long terraces the grottoes were the same, like shop-window displays.

On the train, one stop down, Philip slid lower in his seat, his knees resting on the black plastic back of the seat in front. Some of Minty's mob had got on and were sitting further along the carriage. Their conversation drifted lazily back with their aftershave.

"I'm gonna fuck the shit out of her."

"Bollocks. You'll spew again. Boys, he spewed last time."

"Fuck you, arsehole."

"The Gelli boys'll be down there tonight."

"Let 'em fucking be there."

"They're soft as shit, Lufty and all them."

"I know: Enko goes down after one punch."

"I know that."

They got off four stops later, in Tonypandy. Philip looked through the window, back up the valley. The sky was dark grey. He looked ahead, to the distant gap where the land flattened out. It was completely black. "I'm travelling into the night," he wrote in his book.

Dumfries Street was over a hundred houses long. Claire was near the top, where she would turn and cross the road. She practised wrinkling her nose, for the play. It was her own idea, something to bring to the role, to make her more like a squirrel. The trick was to look cute but not dumb. She liked the play. Jimmy was a bully-boy bastard, but she understood why. Claire only wished that Alison had a stronger personality. Not like Helena, but different again. Jimmy talked about his friend, who could make a bus ride an adventure. That's the kind of woman Jimmy needed. Patience and sympathy were no good. Confrontation didn't work. You had to take him where he didn't usually go. Claire loved thinking things through like that, usually when she was walking somewhere. She sometimes stepped in dog-shit, though. You had to keep your eyes open.

Seven stops away, further into the dark, Philip had written a poem. It was called 'After Love':

I looked across at
an afternoon, blue;
my feet were deep
in chicken bones.
The metal steps
cried rust,
collapsed.
I was stranded
on the roof.

He'd gone to sit in the smoking section, a dirty booth at the front of the train. Down here, seven stops down, the view started to change. There were thousands of things out in the dark; street lights, car lights, shop neon, tree silhouettes, a fat moth that bounced off the window, shady buildings, suggestions of hills – everything was sliding along. He felt as though he were swimming through the universes. He tried to write a poem about it, called 'Nite Train', but scribbled it out and drew the 2-Tone logo instead.

The partition wall between the bedrooms made a hollow sound when you punched it. It also shook. Jason had been punching it for a while now. His Kinder Egg toys jumped on the CD player. He smiled.

"Right, I'm off then," his father called.

"OK, see you."

There was a pause. His father must be lingering in the hall.

"There's supposed to be a good film on later" he called.

"Great," Jason said.

"Right, see you later then."

"See you."

Footsteps, then the front door opening and closing. Jason bounced off the bed and into the chair, thumping his elbow.

"Fuck."

He went through to the living room, poured himself a drink and picked up the phone.

"Hello, is Martin Greaves there?" he said.

"I'll just go and get him."

Jason lit a fag. *Family Fortunes* was on.

"Hello?" said Martin Greaves.

"Hi, it's Jason."

"Erm..."

"Jason Morgan, I was speaking to you on Monday. About housing."

"Sorry, this is going to sound really ignorant, but can you remind me?"

"Yeah, right, I phoned you at your office on Monday, about housing. Getting a flat."

"Housing for the Disabled?"

"Yeah, that."

"Ah, right. Sorry about that, it's just that I've taken on so many different things lately, it's sometimes difficult to remember which hat I'm wearing. Right, so you were enquiring about Housing for the Disabled?"

"Yeah, and you said you were off to Wrexham for the rest of the week, and gave me your home number."

"OK then, Jason, let me take a few details off you."

"Well, I'm 21 and I'd like a flat please."

Martin chuckled.

"I'll see what I can do," he laughed.

"Great," Jason said, and took a drink.

"Is it for yourself?"

"Yes."

"So you're disabled?"

"Uh-huh."

"OK Jason, well what kind of extent of disability are we talking about here? I'm thinking in terms of special needs."

"I'm paraplegic. Possibly alcoholic. In terms of special needs, think in terms of a good hard shag."

Martin chuckled again.

"Well, don't we all, eh?" he said.

Jason echoed his laugh.

"You seem to be doing all right for yourself," he said.

"Sorry?"

"The bird who answered the phone. Sounded a bit foxy, I reckon." Jason blew out smoke, grinning, knowing just how childish he was being.

"Yeah, that's my wife," Martin said. "And as for foxy – well, I think so, yes."

The man was a Weeble – he wobbled but he didn't fall down. Jason took a swig of whiskey and, as it was burning down, said, "Would you ever go out with a cripple?"

"I do, my wife."

Jason started to laugh. "Oh shit, sorry mate. I had no idea," he said.

"That's OK, we're all cripples together here."

In the school hall Ben Wilmott went through his paces as Jimmy. It was chilly without the heating on, and Claire pulled her sleeves over her hands. Ben Wilmott tried to look as though his best friend had just died in his arms and his pregnant wife had left him.

"Oh, how could she be so bloody wet!" he shouted. "Deep loving need! That makes me puke!"

He crossed to the right of the stage.

"She couldn't say 'You rotten bastard! I hate your guts, I'm clearing out, and I hope you rot!' No, she has to make a polite emotional mess out of it!" he screeched.

Mr Hayhurst stopped him.

"I think, Ben, that you're in danger of peaking too soon," he said. "You need to keep that simmering intensity, that rage, you need to keep that going for another two pages."

"Mmm, yeah, right," Ben said. He started again.

Claire looked at his chin, his jawline. There was something unconvincing about that part of his face. It looked young somehow, though Ben was older than she was. She visualised the way Jason's jaw curved down from his ear. There were a few licks of his brown hair curling around his neck.

She leaned back in the chair, picking at the paint on its metal legs. It flaked off and fell to the wooden floor. Ben Wilmott waved his arms around and stamped. Jason could be Jimmy. Her brother could be Cliff. And she'd be Alison, but she'd be Claire as well, so the play would go differently. She toyed with her laces.

Philip got off the train, fifteen stops away at Cardiff Central. He bought a ticket for Newport, on the London train, then lit a fag and sat down for the twenty minute wait. Tall buildings winked darkly at him through the gaps. The breeze smelt of city – carbon monoxide and layered grime. There were voices in the distance, shouting and singing.

A family occupied the next bench, the type that appeared in BBC2 documentaries about infertility treatment. They were whispering about the funeral they'd been to. The daughter wore a neck brace and had some teeth missing.

On the other side, some immaculately dressed goths were posing with a purple guitar. They glanced over at Philip's DIY ensemble, his ripped jeans and gelled hair. They must have a few quid to dress like that, and plenty of time on their hands. He stared back at them and, one by one, they all looked away. He ran his hand through his greasy hair, smirking. A monkey-faced commuter caught his eye, and he looked away too.

Horns beeped on some arterial road, and Philip saw a seagull glide past the black, shining windows of an office block. Away down the track, the Inter City was hurtling through the wind, on its way from Swansea.

In the living room, Jason was looking into his glass. The smooth sides, shallow, drip, dripping with ice, bulged, flat, cool, smashed, the lip, lapped, empty. He re-filled it.

The rehearsal room toilets, and Claire sat in a cubicle, thinking about Jason, his big arms, his big eyes, red and tired in the kitchen at night, but always darting around, pecking at her, yes, pecking at her body. She hugged herself, then felt stupid. But yes, it was true, she wanted to feel Jason's arms around her, not just touching her hand, but crushing her ribs with his strength and his desperation. Her teeth clenched in a grin, her eyes narrow. She wanted him in her room, not in Philip's, and not on the floor but in her bed, right next to her. When it came her turn to act, she found she had to concentrate to remember the lines.

Philip got off the bus in Westfield Crescent, a smart cul-de-sac near the top of a rise with a view of the city lights in the distance. He marched along the road and found number 32. Jason and his father lived in the downstairs flat. Philip pushed the Morgan buzzer. It was starting to get cold. He stamped his feet, watched his breath steam out into the night. The intercom clicked.

"Hello?"

"Jason?"

"Yeah?"

"It's me."

The intercom crackled.

"Jason?"

"Yeah?"

"Jason, it's me."

"Who?"

"Philip."

"Phil?"

"Oh, for fuck's sake Jason, open the door."

"Hang on, I'll open the door."

Pissed again, Philip thought. The door opened and he walked through to the living room. The gas fire was on full, and some ITV drama about a detective was blaring from the television. Philip walked up behind the settee, and Jason's head popped up.

"Phil, how's it going?"

"OK, mate. You?"

Jason was stretched out on the grey leather, his feet sticking out over the end. He was wearing a pair of really expensive trainers.

"I'm feeling mellow, at the moment," he said. "What are you doing here?"

"I got your letter. Thought I'd come and visit."

"So you didn't think of ringing first?"

"What?"

"I might have been out." He reached over to the coffee table, which was laden with cigarettes, whiskey, glasses and three remote controls. He lit a fag.

"Your letter made me think you'd be in."

"Perceptive," Jason said, as Philip came and stood in front of the fire. "Christ, what happened to you on the way?"

"My hair, you mean?"

"Your hair, your jeans, the plaster on your head..."

"I thought I'd get dressed up a bit."

"To come and see me?"

Philip shrugged. "I thought we could go out. Have a laugh."

Jason frowned, struggled to sit up, looked at Philip. "Did you see *Casualty* last week?"

"What, that thing about the hospital? No."

"There was a fire at a gig."

"Yeah?"

"Yeah."

Philip still hadn't taken his jacket off.

"It was in this club," Jason said, "and this band was on. It was like the BBC's idea of an indie band, right? Anyway, the human interest angle focused on this group of friends at the gig, mates, yeah? And they were like the BBC's idea of alternative youth culture, you know? Lots of black and all that. A bit like you look now."

The backs of Philip's legs were getting hot from the fire. He moved to the windowsill.

"Yeah, carry on," he said.

"OK, so one of the mates was in a wheelchair. He was white, but he had dreadlocks. Wore a leather jacket. Studs. Biker boots. With me?"

"Go on."

"Well, a fire happens. The unscrupulous club owner has ignored the fire regulations. In the confusion, one of the friends gets lost, collapses in the smoke. All the others get outside, but the wheelchair guy realises there's one missing. Spins the chair around, goes back into the fire, rescues his friend, comes out with him on his lap."

"Is this going anywhere?"

"No. Right, so – back at the hospital they all troop past the bourgeoisie in the waiting room, looking like a travelling freak show – all chains and body piercings and Mr Dreadlocks in the wheelchair all smoke-damaged. The poshoes turn up their noses, obviously thinking they've been up to no good – possibly thinking in terms of Satan worshippers whose ceremony got out of hand. But all the casualty people know, and we know, they're just a bunch of friends making their own way in this crazy old world of ours."

"We know the wheelchair guy is a true friend, and a brave and courageous one. Moral – appearances don't matter, it's what's inside that counts."

Jason reached for the bottle and poured the last of the whiskey into his glass.

"Well," Philip said, "thanks for telling me the plot of last week's *Casualty*."

"That's OK."

Philip sighed. "Was there a point, by the way?"

"The wheelchair guy was where he wanted to be, right? So he was happy." Jason said.

Philip rubbed his eyes. He'd been awake since 6.30 that morning.

"Jason," he said, "please, please, please get to the point."

"It's bollocks, that's the point."

"It's only telly."

"It's not, it's everything." He flared up like a match, angry lines slashing his forehead.

"When you achieve X it will cancel out everything and you'll be happy." He said it as though quoting from some textbook on contentment. "But it's bullshit – you carry it with you," he hissed, looking away from Philip at the empty bottle.

"What have you done?" Philip asked.

"What the fuck do you mean?"

"You've tried something, haven't you? And it hasn't worked."

Jason raised his eyebrows equivocally. "TJ's", he said.

"Pardon me?"

"The club. You must have heard of it, for Christ's sake."

"Yeah, yeah."

"Well, I went there. Saw some bands. Came home. On my own. Went to bed."

"That's it."

"And then this episode of Casualty last week, just to rub it in." Philip nodded.

"All that bullshit," Jason said.

Philip shook his head. "That's a motherfucker of a coincidence."

"No, it's just the usual. Another funny little prank, just to ram the point home. You with me?"

"God?"

"Or whatever."

Philip scratched his head. "So you don't want to go out then?"

Jason sighed and looked at his watch. "It's a bit late. It'll take at least half an hour to get into town and I'm half pissed anyway."

Philip took off his jacket and sat down. "You shouldn't let these things get to you so much."

Jason laughed. "Look who's talking. I mean, what are you doing up here? You're on the run, aren't you?"

Philip shrugged again. "Do you think appearance matters?"

"Of course it does. Why have you done yourself up like that? It means something, doesn't it? To you, at least. And, you hope, to me."

Phil sat in the armchair, his green eyes wide, his arms lolling helplessly. Jason looked over at his friend with his new hairstyle wilting in the heat, and his smile was gentle.

"I always have this effect on people," he said. "Phil, look, have a drink with me? A little drinkie? C'mon, you old bastard, give us a smile, eh? You're here now. Have a drink and a fag."

"I don't smoke," Philip said.

"You do."

"Yeah, you're right. How do you do that?"

"Nature has compensated me for my useless body, to the tune of vastly enhanced mental powers," Jason drawled, "which don't, by the way, include telekinesis, so you might like to get a new bottle from that cabinet over there before we both die of thirst and that's an end to the whole bloody thing."

Philip laughed and got the drink. It was always like this when they met up. Jason was spiky as hell for a while, then he seemed to relax.

Philip was so relaxed he stayed all weekend and, when it came time for work on Monday, he was fast asleep on Jason's floor. Just before crashing out at six in the morning, Jason put a Cocteau Twins CD on.

"I've stuck it on repeat," Jason said, "so if we wake up at all we'll be lulled back to sleep again."

"This is great," Philip murmured, his eyes shut. "You'll have to come down my place next time."

Jason eased his trainers off and stretched out on his bed. "Can't wait," he grinned.

6. DECEMBER 1992.

Claire dialled the number her teacher had given her. It rang eighteen times before being picked up.

Kelvin: Hello, Rhondda Community Arts Workshop.

Claire: Hello, can I speak to Kelvin Nussbaum, please?

Kelvin: Speaking.

Claire: Hi, my name's Claire McKay. I'm doing GCSE Drama at Treorchy Comprehensive and my teacher, Colin Hayhurst, suggested I give you a ring.

Kelvin: Yeah, right, I remember Colin saying something about this, yeah. You're the girl who's turning all the heads.

Claire: Well, I don't know...

Kelvin: Yeah, you were in the paper, weren't you? You won the Clayton Linton Young Playwright Award, didn't you?

Claire: Yes, I did. Anyway, the idea was that I come down and help put on some kind of production at the theatre.

Kelvin: Yeah, I mean, I think it's an excellent idea. What we're trying to do is provide a kind of community-based programme of arts activities, and we're particularly interested in catering for the young people in the area.

Claire: Yeah, right.

Kelvin: So, I mean, from my point of view, I'd love to see young people like yourself taking on a project, something that interests them, and is based on their experience. I mean, we've got all the facilities and stuff here, but I'd kind of like to give the creative reins over to you, Claire, if you see what I mean. How does that sort of thing sound to you?

Claire: Great, yeah. Really exciting. I'm hoping to study drama at university.

Kelvin: Sure, well, this could be a great experience for you.

Claire: I'm really looking forward to it.

Kelvin: Great, that's excellent. Right, well I can fix something up with Colin, and you can come down and have a chat. Thrash a few things out.

Claire: OK then, I'll do that.

Kelvin: I mean – I'm just trying to think of what kind of thing we can set up here. We do a lot of stuff with youngsters, as I said, and we also work with unemployed people, people with disabilities, you know, that sort of thing. I think they get a lot from it.

Claire: I'm sure they do.

Kelvin: Obviously we'll work out what you want to do, what sort of themes you want to be dealing with when we meet up. But if you've got any ideas, any people you want to involve, go ahead.

Claire: OK, I'll do that.

Kelvin: I mean, it's important to let people speak for themselves who wouldn't normally have the chance, you know. I mean, the unemployed, y'know, people who slipped through the net, sort of thing, at school, I mean, and disabled people, they've got all kinds of things to say, and I think it's important we hear them.

Claire: Yeah, absolutely.

Kelvin: OK then, Claire, I'll speak to you soon then.

Claire: Great. Thanks a lot.

Kelvin: Yeah, no problem. Bye bye now.

Claire: So long.

She put the phone down.

It was a con how she dragged him and Philip into the thing, Jason later thought. But he was drunk all the time, and just wanted anything other than have to go home to his mother or his father, or the empty flat Martin said was being done up ready for him. So he'd do anything, go anywhere, as long as there were people there he could bump into and swear at to keep him awake.

And Claire knew all this, and didn't have to do a thing, just a look and a word maybe, she was such a smooth operator. A teenage girl with a brain like a computer processor.

It started when Jason came for a festive visit. The night before, in the pub, someone tried to drape tinsel over his chair and he told her to stuff it up her arse. Philip, dressed like a mourner at the world's funeral, flinched. But there was no more avoiding it, no more pushing Jason away from the trouble he caused. Philip had chosen sides long since. Since he stayed up Jason's that time, after that office party. He'd never gone back to work. This was what he did now.

So when Minty passed him in the pub last night, and looked at him like an old tomcat looks at a clockwork mouse, Philip slouched against the fag machine, arching his eyebrows, his face wide open: problem, mate? And Minty pushed his way past to the toilets and Philip grinned like a bastard. He was as honest as Jason now.

Then it was Thursday, and Val and Joan had gone back to work, saving their leave for Jersey in the summer. Philip and Jason were watching *Digby, the Biggest Dog in the World*, with a cocktail each, mixed from leftovers.

"They marketed Jim Dale as a sex symbol originally," Philip said, "in the mould of Cliff Richard, or that gormless twat with the teeth."

Jason was wearing his Christmas present from Claire, a vaguely ethnic string and bead necklace. It coiled around his big neck, drew attention to his square jaw, his prominent vein.

"What gormless twat?" he asked.

"You know – *Little White Bull*."

"Oh yeah, Billy Steele."

Claire came in with her coat on and got some handkerchiefs from the box.

"Tommy, I think," she said.

"Billy Tommy?" Philip frowned into his drink.

"Off out again?" Jason said.

"Yeah, concept meeting."

"What, at the theatre?"

"The Park and Dare, yeah, we're kicking a few ideas around."

"Who's we?"

"Kelvin, Dee-Dee, Poul, a couple of the others. Most of them aren't back off their Christmas holidays yet, they're still at home."

"At home?"

"England."

"Oh."

Philip was engrossed in the film and didn't see Claire wink at Jason as she left. Jason was quiet for a while. Then he said, "Hey Phil."

"Yeah?"

"Let's go out."

"Where to?'

"I don't know, just for a walk. We'll get a bottle on the way."

"OK, hang on," Philip sighed.

In the lane a group of teenagers squatted. Claire kept her eyes on the pavement as she passed. They watched her go, then huddled together again. It was a strange day – although the sun was hidden, the world seemed bleached. A white Christmas. Dirty white really.

Claire heard the pssst of an aerosol can from the lane and some giggles. Kelvin should be here now, he'd talk to them. He never went up this road though. He drove up from Cardiff, left his car by the bottle bank in the library car-park, and walked across to the theatre. He looked kind of cool, with his jacket blowing around him. But he would never come along this road. Kelvin probably thought the whole valley looked like the inside of a community centre. Yellowed posters about Chile and stained cups behind radiators. He went back home to Exeter on the weekends. But he was OK, Kelvin. He was right, really, in what he said. And he knew so many people.

She walked up to the side entrance of the theatre, past a huge graffiti swastika with an anarchy symbol combined into its design. A slogan underneath read, "Be a man, join the Klan."

When she got into the corridor, Kelvin's dog bounded up to her and broke wind.

"Glyndwr!" came Kelvin's voice.

The dog was named after the real Prince of Wales. Kelvin had picked her up from a dog's home in Cardiff and changed her name from Sally. He pronounced it Glendower. The flatulent bitch rarely responded.

"Claire, hi," Kelvin said. "Listen, I want to produce some anger today."

"Anger. Right," Claire said.

"It might get a bit heavy actually," Kelvin said, "so be ready for anything."

He grinned.

A long, sad fart echoed from Glyndwr's bowel.

"OK, let's go," Kelvin said, leading Claire into the rehearsal room.

"You go around with that spastic, don't you?"

"Pardon me?" Philip said.

Jason was inside Spar getting some Bacardi. A group of monkey-faced teenagers milled around outside.

"That spastic," one of them said. "You go around with him."

"Do I?"

"Yeah, fucking right."

"My brother, you mean?" Philip asked.

"Is he your brother?" one kid asked.

"Is that why you go around with him?" another said.

"Have you got to look after him?"

"Is he mental?"

"Have you got a fag?"

Jason appeared, screwing the top off a bottle. He looked at the group clustered around Phil. They squinted at him, the boss-monkey fiddling with a Stanley knife blade.

"You know when you go to bed at night," Jason said, "and take your clothes off?"

A red Escort roared along the road, and the four baseball caps inside turned to fix on Philip, until the car was gone.

"Do you find little flakes of shit in your pants?" Jason said.

Philip spluttered on his fag.

"You're mental, mate," the boss-monkey said.

"Fucking right," Jason grinned. "And I eat razor blades."

"Clear a path, monkey-boys," Philip said, pushing through the group. "We've got an appointment with Jesus."

"Yeah, we're going to rip his pubes out," Jason snarled, following his friend.

"You can have them, if you like," Philip said. "The Sacred

Pubes, I mean. They might come in handy at your next circle-jerk up the woods."

Jason passed him the bottle and he took a swig. When they were ten yards away, the monkey-boss shouted, "I bet you two bum each other!"

"Nah," Philip called, "we find little monkey-faced boys and do it to them."

Jason burst out laughing.

"Yeah, and then we stab them," he shouted.

They were circling Treorchy, heading sort of down, Philip thought, down towards Stag Square. They were going down, all right, Jason thought, down to the theatre. The Bacardi was definitely going down.

The road they were on was a dark twin, according to Philip. It ran exactly parallel to the main road through Treorchy, but separated from it by seven streets, the way the rungs separate both sides of a ladder.

The High Street was full of supermarkets, chemists, newsagents, pubs, where smiling men in lumberjack shirts shouted insults at each other.

The nameless back road followed its contours exactly, every last dip and curve. But instead of supermarkets it had skips overflowing with PVC window frames. The pavements were overgrown with grass, and people took their dogs to shit there. A murky garage puked injured BMWs a thousand yards along the road, where they squatted in oil and windscreen crystals. At the bottom of the High Street was the huge but cosy old Stag Hotel. Its twin mirrored it with an abattoir.

Old men sat on benches along the road, talking of levels, drams, dust, suicides. Philip called this tree-lined road 'The Boulevard', and loved to walk it. People passing through town in their caravans didn't know it was there, and they didn't care.

Philip and Jason had cut through a lane to join this road, and they came upon a gang of teenagers hiding in an alcove.

"Don't mind us." Jason waved the bottle.

"I know you." One of the kids stood up, looking at Jason. "Yeah?"

Acne and bumfluff hid the lower half of his face like a veil.

He burped and there was a smell of butane. He was wearing a
Father Christmas hat.

"You gave me a fag before."

"Before what?" Jason said.

"Ages ago. By the library. You were with him." He pointed
at Philip.

"Oh yeah, I remember," Philip said. "It was your birthday."

"Yeah," the kid said.

"So what are you up to now, then?" Jason asked.

"Whippets, like," the kid said, slipping the air freshener out
of his bomber jacket.

"What?" Jason frowned.

The kid demonstrated, pressing the aerosol button and
sniffing the swift burst of propellant.

"Oh, right," Jason said. "We call it whiffing where I come
from."

The gang was shuffling around in the alcove. The blank
back windows of the houses looked straight past them. One kid
was playing a Gameboy.

"It's good when you're high, playing that," said the kid they
knew. "It's like you're going into it, like."

"I know that, it's mad as fuck," another kid agreed, sticking
a tampon in his mouth and pretending to smoke it.

"Can I offer you a light?" Jason drawled.

"Aye, go on then," the kid grinned.

Jason took out his lighter and held it to the end of the
tampon. It lit, pouring with smoke, and the kid marched
around, a tycoon with a fat cigar.

"Look boys, I'm the fucking Prime Minister," he laughed.
When the flames got too close to his face he took the tampon
out of his mouth, and held it between his fingers. The kid they
knew sprayed air freshener on to the flame. The chemical
caught fire, and a jet of flame ripped through the air, just past
Jason's shoulder.

The kid dropped the tampon fast, blowing on his fingers.

"Fucking hell Titch, you mental cunt," he squeaked.

Titch laughed. "Like a fucking flamethrower," he said.

Jason passed the bottle to Philip, who took a swig to take

away the mixed chemical smells, which he could taste in his throat. Then they started to move off down the lane.

"Where you off then?" Titch called.

"Just sniff your gas," Jason said.

In the library car-park, in the shadow of the theatre, Philip slumped to the floor, reading a heavily tea-stained *Times Literary Supplement*.

"Get up, you dozy tit," Jason said. "I haven't finished."

"I'm having a fucking read, ain't I?" Philip said.

"Do that after. Help me find some wank-fodder."

The slots of the paper-recycling skip were just too high for Jason to reach. He needed Philip to lift him.

"Come on, Phil, for fuck's sake," Jason whined. "I can't trust you to do the job properly." He made a sulky scratch along a Nissan Micra with his front door key.

"All right, hang on." Philip put down his paper and came over.

Jason put his feet on the ground, and Philip lifted him from behind into an upright position. Jason held on to the skip, stuck his arms through the gap, and started rummaging around. Philip held him in place with one hand on the scruff of his neck, and tried to light a fag with the other.

Unable to look through the gap at what he was doing, Jason was grabbing anything that felt glossy, passing it from one hand to the other, and throwing it out of the skip. A few magazines had already landed on the floor while Philip was trying to find his lighter.

"Philip, hey Philip, what's happening?" Jason said.

"Hold on, man, hold on," Philip said. "Christ."

"Well, what's the score so far?"

"A *TV Times*, three issues of *Which* magazine, *Bella*, *Best*, *Hello*, *TV Times* again, *The Journal of Medical Health*, a *Teenage Mutant Hero Turtles* comic, and another *TV Times*." Philip's hand was starting to feel cramped. "Jason, my hand's going dead," he said.

"Just a few more," Jason said.

"Well, I'm going to have to change hands then. Hold on."

Philip leaned against Jason, squashing him against the greasy metal skip, and took his hand away. He flexed his fingers.

"Come on, Phil, there's shit all over this skip," Jason said.

Philip stuck out his other arm and grabbed Jason's collar.

"OK, carry on," Philip said.

More magazines came fluttering out of the skip.

"Right, we've got...an advertising supplement for holidays in the Cotswolds. *TV* bloody *Times*, again. Another *Journal of Medical Health*. I didn't know we had any doctors living in Treorchy. Perhaps we don't – just some weirdo. What else? Well, a copy of *Q* with a big piece on the making of *Sergeant Pepper* in it. We'll have that. *Cosmopolitan* – we'll have that for the quiz. A copy of *Puzzle Monthly* that someone's been working out anagrams on the front of. Another bloody *TV Times*! I wish you'd – ah, looks like you've hit pay-dirt, Jase."

"What? What is it?"

"*Health and Efficiency*."

"What?"

"You know, that nudist magazine."

"Better than fuck all, I suppose."

Jason wrestled his arms out of the skip, Philip helped him slump back into the chair.

He started flipping through *Health and Efficiency*, grimacing.

"Oh Christ, this is a bit fucking grim."

Philip laughed as Jason pointed out a naked man reading Proust in a rocking chair, his genitals somehow reminiscent of Woody Allen.

A police car cruised into the car park. A pair of police helmets turned slowly in their direction. The car circled and stopped by the bottle bank. Two policemen got out. A chunky, unshaven bloke in a wheelchair was reading a magazine with two naked women on the front. There were flakes of rust on his sleeves. A bottle of Bacardi was sticking up between his legs. Next to him a skinny teenager with a mop of dyed black hair crouched in a pile of magazines, a fag between his lips. They were both giggling. One of the policemen coughed, and they both looked up.

"Hello?" said the skinny one.

After the policemen watched them put all the magazines back, they escorted them from the car park. As they got to the corner, Philip noticed a middle-aged man in the corner house peering through the net curtain.

"Why don't they catch some real criminals?" Jason said.

"Yeah, like Ronnie Biggs, or the Kray Twins."

"Or Raffles."

"Or Hitler."

"Or Hamburglar. You know, Ronald McDonald's enemy."

Laughing, they came out onto Dyfodwg Street, and the police car disappeared. Four men, leaning on a red Escort, watched it go.

"Fuck me, it's the freakshow."

Philip gave Minty a crooked smile. All right, mate?"

But Minty was looking at Jason. "Why do you always make a prick of yourself?"

"When?" Jason said, frowning.

"Up the pub. Don't he, boys?"

The boys agreed.

"See?" said Minty. "You're a pain in the arse."

He was a handsome bloke, Minty. He had that firm jawline you always hear about, and the same expensive trainers that Jason wore. His car was fuel-injected. A few Income Support forms lay on the dashboard.

"You don't even live here," Minty said.

Jason did a long sigh. "You're boring," he said.

Philip turned his head away sharply, then forced himself to turn it back.

Minty made a disgusted face and turned his back on them. "You better watch your step," he said.

Minty's boys kept their eyes on them as they passed by. Then they all got in the car.

The Escort cruised past them, heading for the main road. Minty kept his eyes on the road, but the others watched Philip and Jason. One, with an earnest expression, lifted his middle finger.

"Fucking pigs," Jason muttered.

In the calm shadows of Paolo's cafe, opposite the theatre,

Jason was quiet. Across the road some people were taking props out of a small van and into the building. Philip was glad of the sit down, he felt quite pissed. He looked around Paolo's, at all the wood-effect formica.

"It's funny," he said, "but I know more types of plastic than types of tree."

A man in a flowing black coat came down the steps of the theatre, and started taking chairs out of the van.

At the back of the cafe, two girls and a boy, around Phil's age, sniggered as they stared over. The boy kept saying, "Oi," – a bit louder each time, testing his nerve. The two girls, one blond and one dark, giggled into their Diet Cokes.

"Polystyrene, polyurethane, formica, polyvinylchloride, or PVC," Phil said, sipping his coffee.

Then Claire emerged from the archway and skipped down the steps. She had her hair in a ponytail today. It bounced against her shoulders as she came down the steps.

The boy on the back table took some chewing gum out of his mouth.

"I think bakelite was one of the first plastics."

The man in the coat came down the steps and joined Claire. She was smiling and laughing as she helped him carry a table out of the van.

The boy rolled his chewing gum into a ball on his thumb and took aim.

"There's all this shit about bio-degradable materials now," Phil was saying, "but I still reckon plastic's cool."

Claire and the man disappeared through the arch. The chewing gum ball shot past Jason's face, bounced off the window, and fell on the table in front of him. The boy and the girls turned their backs, grinning madly.

Jason picked up the sticky gumball.

"Let's go to the theatre," he murmured.

When they got to the door, Jason stopped and turned.

"Oi, wanker." Jason was a violent thug. You could hear it in his voice.

The boy looked around. The girls' blue eyes were wide.

"Do that again and I'll break your fucking neck." And Jason

flicked the chewing gum ball the entire length of Paolo's, over six tables and an old man with a damaged larynx, and it hit the boy on the side of his head. Philip grinned. Jason was fucking unbelievable.

They hit the street and started across the road. As Philip dragged Jason up the steps into the theatre he saw the two girls leaning in the cafe doorway. The boy was walking away, drawing on a fag. The girls smiled at Philip and Jason as they disappeared through the archway. Philip gave them a wink.

Kelvin shook his head.

"I think we're being too analytical about this. What I think we should do is just sort of let it flow for a bit. Just improvise on the idea of anger, of frustration."

He ran his hands through his hair, and motioned everyone back. Claire perched on a table. Kelvin started improvising.

In the corridor, Glyndwr came ambling up to Phil and Jason.

"Hello, boy," Philip said.

Glyndwr flinched, turned, got dizzy, and bumped into Jason's chair. They laughed.

"What a crap dog!" Philip said.

"Hey, listen," Jason said.

They shut up. They could hear a voice.

"Ah, fuck it," the voice was shouting. "I don't know what I want, I just know that I don't want this. Every night I go out and get pissed. I'm trying to have fun, but I know I'm just blocking it out. And every morning it's there again. It's there in the pub, with all the lads. It's there in the dole office. It's always there. And I don't know what the fuck to call it!"

"He don't know what the fuck to call it," Jason said.

"Let's go and see if we can help him," Philip said.

They started off down the corridor again, Glyndwr tagging along.

"I can't name it, I can't get it out, I just want to shout, and smash everything up – and it's all because I can't say what I mean!" The voice again, coming from behind a half-open door.

"We're bound to be able to help," Philip said. "I know loads of words."

He was unsteady on his feet, bumping off the wall occasionally. Jason was better, he was just whistling as he wheeled himself along.

"They say I need a job," the voice continued. "What I really need is – Claire, help me: what do I need?"

"Um, some fun?"

Jason sped up, and pushed the door open. He barged through, followed by Philip.

"Hello," Philip said.

"Hi." Claire waved.

"Oh, right, these are friends of yours, are they Claire?" Kelvin asked.

He was standing in the middle of the room.

"That's my brother, Phil, and that's his friend, Jason," Claire said. "This is Kelvin, this is Dee-Dee, and Poul," she added.

"Hi Phil, Jason," Kelvin said.

"Hello, how are you?" Philip said, and sat down heavily on a chair. His suede boots were covered in dust, and his hair had flopped badly.

"It's good that you've dropped by," Kelvin said.

Jason had his surly face on, and was chewing a fingernail he'd bitten off earlier. There were still flakes of rust on his jacket. He pulled out the Bacardi bottle and poured the last drops down his throat.

"Why?" he said, and threw the bottle across the room at the overflowing bin. It hit the side and the whole lot fell over.

"Jason," Claire said.

"Sorry 'bout that," Jason shrugged.

Philip laughed at him.

"Have you come to join in then?" Kelvin asked.

Jason had his face shut, and Philip looked blank and dazed.

"We'd be really happy to have you here," Kelvin said. "No pressure, but what we're trying to do might be up your street."

"Yeah, turn left at the abattoir," Philip giggled.

Claire looked at her brother. She knew the street he was talking about.

Kelvin only got annoyed, though, when piss started pouring through the letterbox.

Jason and Philip saw it first, and started giggling to each other.

"Art can have a tremendous healing and unifying power," Kelvin was saying. "That's what community art is all about. Sorry – Phil, Jason: is there something you want to contribute? Only it's a little distracting having you two tittering away there."

Kelvin followed their eyes to the door. It was spattering on the carpet tiles.

"Jesus Christ!" Kelvin jumped up and ran for the door. The pissing stopped, and footsteps were heard. Kelvin opened the door. They'd gone.

He made a show of looking for them, spreading the piss around. Jason and Phil watched eagerly as he turned to face the group. Claire, who had hidden a smile behind her script, put on a serious face. Kelvin's colleagues sighed. He stood glaring at them all. One arm was outstretched, pointing at the doorway. The breeze made his hair flap around his ears.

"That's exactly what I'm talking about," he exclaimed.

His dog wandered out from under the desk and started sniffing the piss.

"Those kids are what I'm talking about," he raged. "They want to piss over everything. Fine. That's just fine by me."

Dee-Dee cleared her throat. Kelvin's arm was still stuck out, quivering.

His dog started licking the piss.

"Glyndwr," Kelvin yelled. "Fuck off!"

7. MARCH 1993.

So they got involved with Claire's project. Jason had to come to Treorchy quite often, for the concept meetings, the rehearsals. Philip was given the script to write, and Claire was the director. Kelvin Nussbaum brought his colleagues Dee-Dee French and Poul Artess in. Kids kept stuffing empty cider bottles through the windows and running off.

Kelvin wished they'd just come in once, see what it was all about, perhaps get involved. He also wished they hadn't scratched his Nissan Micra.

Philip's eighteenth birthday came and went. Morrissey brought out another solo album. The weather was quite mild. Three months on and none of the script was written.

"Look," he said, "just tell me what you want me to write and I'll write it."

"I've already told you," Claire said.

"Yeah, but it didn't make any sense."

"Yes it did. You just didn't understand."

Jason loved listening to them argue. Their voices came to sound the same, the ends of their sentences went high and flutey.

"Claire, why don't you read Phil your notes," Dee-Dee said.

"A surreal, futuristic setting, but based on contemporary valleys life," Claire read.

"Characters appear as representatives of different urban tribes. They are alienated from each other as well as from the world in general. Despite their differences, the ending reveals a recognition of their shared plight, and a unity of purpose."

Claire looked at Philip.

"That's it, is it?" Philip asked.

"Can you do it or not?" Claire said.

"Of course he can do it," Dee-Dee smiled. "He's a wunder-kind, aren't you Phil?"

Philip tried an ironic smile and looked away. He'd made the mistake of mentioning Nietzche to Dee-Dee within minutes of meeting her. He was paying for it now.

"Yes, OK, I can do it, leave it to me."

"Right, so we can expect to see something we can work on?" Kelvin said.

"Soon," Philip said, "Really soon."

"Good. Now – Jason."

"Yeah?"

"Jason. Jason, Jason, Jason, Jason," Kelvin mused, chewing the top of his overhead projector pen.

"Yeah?" Jason said.

"I think it's time we sorted out your role in this."

Jason sighed massively.

"Look, Jase, it's like this," Claire said. "You're one of the urban tribes."

"Which one?" Jason asked.

"Well," said Claire, "you, well, you represent the disabled." Their eyes met, but Claire glanced down at her folder.

"Why?" Philip's voice was belligerent. "Why can't he represent, I don't know, alcoholics? Or obnoxious people in general?"

"Piss off, Phil," Jason said, quietly.

"See? Obnoxious."

"I take your point, Phil, but people will be automatically drawn to the wheelchair," Kelvin said. "So why not use that?"

"Look Jason," Dee-Dee said, "it's up to you. There's no pressure. This project is about everyone involved in it finding what they want to say, and the way they want to say it. So it has to be your decision."

Jason was still looking at Claire. Her eyes came slowly up from the folder. They were narrow, and shone green. Like the lights on a computer that show it's on-line. He could just fucking hit her. She'd look even cuter with two black eyes, like a little panda. But there was already a churning in his stomach; he felt sick about wanting to hit her. It was nearly over, just like that.

"What do you think, Jase?" she said, and her voice was intimate, just for him.

He had no choice. It was this or back to Newport, to the flat. It was the McKays or nothing.

"Yeah, whatever," he told her.

She, thank fuck, didn't smile. Then he would really have hit her. She nodded seriously; and just as that was starting to piss him off as well, just before she turned back to the group, she gave him a look that was pure sex.

"So that's that sorted then," she said, business-like again. "Phil's going to give us a script by next week –"

"What? Next week?"

"– and the first bit will be Jason's. Because we haven't got anyone else in it yet."

Later, Kelvin started talking about a stage production of Picasso's *Guernica* that he'd done at university, so they packed it in and went to the pub.

The Red Lion was full that night, and Val was happy. It wasn't in a good position for trade, stuck up in Cwmparc, but it had really started to pick up. The owners, Colin and Margaret, were old friends of Val and Joan. Used to own a pub in Bridgend where Val took Joan before they were married. They'd done wonders for The Red Lion. They'd re-decorated the lounge but left the bar the same. That was a good idea. So many of the pubs in the valley were being taken over by the breweries, and they all ended up looking the same. You had different crowds going to different pubs – youngsters' pubs, rough pubs, pubs that did good food. The Lion kept a good mix by only half renovating. The regulars were still comfortable playing pool in the bar, but more people came in the lounge now. Which was good news for Val.

He'd just played *Summertime Blues*, only three chords, and it went well. His wife was in the corner with some friends from work. They'd be up dancing later. Especially Anne. She knew how to have a good time. In more ways than one. He'd heard she fiddled the Social out of four hundred quid when she started back to work, and they still hadn't done her for it. The girls waved over at him. He grinned slyly, smoothing back his quiff.

"This next one is dedicated to Anne over there," he said.

The girls cheered as he started the tape and the electric

piano intro to *Money, Money, Money* came squirting out of the speakers. Joan and her friends laughed, so Anne had to join in. It was all in fun and, anyway, you had to give them a bit of cheek. Young or old, the girls always loved a bit of cheek. Showed you had balls, like.

"*It's a rich man's world,*" Val sang, grinning.

The lounge door opened and his skinny son came in. All in black as usual. He was a lanky streak of piss, like Val had been until after he got married. Claire and Jason followed him in, and those three arts people from the theatre. He wanted a word with them after. A proposition for them.

Claire waved over at him. He gave her a wink, then messed up a chord and stuttered a line. His eyes met Joan's. She was right, he was probably being too flash. Trying to remember that joke he wanted to tell Claire. He concentrated again and drove the song to the end, glad to abandon it now. He rifled through the backing tapes, until he found *It's a Kind of Magic*. It was a good crowd pleaser, to get them back on his side before the break.

While the intro was playing he looked at Claire, who was talking to Jason. They were laughing a lot. The boy was making short work of his pint. Phil was sandwiched between the arts people on one side, and two young girls on the other. He seemed to be talking to both sets of people at the same time, waving his cigarette around, and running his other hand through his black hair. Good job Joan couldn't see him smoking. They were good little kids though, making friends with Jason and everything. Val missed his cue and had to go round again.

Philip squeezed out from the table and went to the fag machine. One of the girls followed him into the corridor.

"What were you on about in there? I couldn't understand a word," the girl said.

"Ah, just some bollocks."

"Them English people seemed, like, interested."

"Sorry, are you Debbie or Helen?"

"Helen."

"Right. So, did your boyfriend get the chewing gum out of his hair?"

"Lufty?" Helen said. "It didn't go in his hair, and he's not my boyfriend."

Philip got his fags and leaned against the wall, facing Helen.

"I couldn't believe your mate did that," Helen said.

"Yeah, well."

"Is he a laugh, like? You know, is he mad, like? Is that why you go around with him?"

Helen was on the move all the time. She was swivelling her heels left and right, making each of her hips stick out in turn. They moved towards Philip before dropping back into place. At the same time she was swaying her shoulders contrapuntally, making her breasts move around inside her white halter top. Finally, her head was tilting from left to right, like an animal listening. Philip decided to stop looking at her body and concentrate on her eyes. They might be less mobile.

"Yeah," Philip said, having forgotten what she'd asked.

"Are you writing this play then?" Helen asked.

"Yeah. It's going to be a nightmare though."

"Why?"

"Well, the first bit I've got to do is for Jason to act. I've got to write stuff for him to say, about being disabled."

Philip seemed to have caught Helen's rhythm. He noticed he was moving as well. Gently pushing himself off the wall, dropping back, pushing himself forward again. It was a tiny movement, but he was doing it again and again and again.

"Well, you are his friend," Helen said, rubbing her bare arm very slowly.

Philip threw the rest of his pint down his neck. This strong lager Dee-Dee bought him was going down a treat. Better than the cheap piss he normally drank. He lit a fag and offered one to Helen. She leaned towards him for a light.

"Is he your boyfriend?" she asked, puffing on her fag, looking up into his eyes.

"Jason?" Philip laughed clouds of smoke. "Christ!"

Helen laughed with him.

"No, he's my father's friend's son," Philip said. "That's how I know him."

"Your father's the singer?"

"Yeah."

"How many of your family's in there?"

"My father. My sister. My mother."

"So you can't get up to anything," Helen grinned, her head on her right shoulder, her left hip pointing at him.

"Well, I'm off before long," he said, casually.

"Where to?"

"For a walk."

"Wait there, I'm just going to the toilet."

Val came and sat in Philip's place, next to Kelvin Nussbaum.

"Really enjoyed the first half," Kelvin said. "You're a talented family."

"Oh, just a couple of songs, nothing special," Val said.

"You've got a fair bit of equipment."

"Aye, it's sort of built up over the years." Val accepted a pint from Glyn.

"So what's this I hear about you keeping my kids off the streets?" Val smiled.

Kelvin chuckled.

"Excuse my ignorance," Val said, "but is it a play you're doing?"

"Basically, yes," Kelvin said. "What we're trying to do is encourage kids from around here to express themselves, y'know, rather than have old farts like me doing it for them."

He smiled happily.

Val nodded. "Any music in it?"

"Well, I mean, Claire's in charge as far as actual content is concerned, but I guess so, yeah."

"The reason I ask is that I thought I could help out, if you like," Val said.

"Ah, right."

"Well, the offer's there, anyway,"

"Yeah, absolutely."

"I can play modern stuff as well. I do Tina Turner in the second half."

"That's —" Caught without an adjective, Kelvin nodded. "Yeah, yeah," he said, carefully.

"Just thought it'd add a bit of atmosphere. Anyway, the offer's there, like." Val leaned across the table to have a word with Glyn about his angina.

Helen was still in the toilets. Philip slouched around the corridor, having got himself and Helen another drink. He fiddled with the bandit, then wandered to the window.

"Fucking Christ," he murmured.

The mountain loomed up in front of him, darker than the night sky. The stars were blotted out. A glacier gone black with age and cynicism. A pair of tiny lights appeared over the top and started moving slowly along the flank, heading down, into the valley.

Philip turned back to the corridor, confusing his eyes with the sudden change in scale. Floor tiles. Fag ends. Bannister. Bandit. Poster. Lounge door. He counted to twenty then span around to the window. The mountain loomed up again, swift, silent and huge. The lights were further down now. This was awe, Philip decided. It was about not letting your eyes get used to things. He decided to look at the corridor for thirty seconds then try it again. He turned.

"What are you doing?" Helen asked.

"Going off my head," Philip smiled.

The community arts people were dancing. As Val pumped out *Simply the Best*, Dee-Dee suddenly grabbed Kelvin's hand and they took to the floor. Poul stayed where he was, puffing on a roll-up, smiling indulgently at everything. His eyes met Jason, and his smile widened. Jason shuffled in his chair. Claire touched his arm.

"You don't look very comfortable."

"Too crowded."

The lounge was packed now, and it would have been difficult for Jason to go anywhere in a hurry.

An old woman wearing beads excuse-me'd her way to Kelvin. He put his arms around her, and she made a swooning face. Everyone laughed. Kelvin did too, looking boyish.

"Prick," Jason muttered.

Claire winced. "You don't mind being in this play, do you?"

Jason sighed, trying to avoid her eyes. Then a peculiar sound started up, underneath the hubbub. It was Poul, singing along to himself.

"You speak the language of love like you know what it means."

"It's just these bloody people," Jason said.

"I haven't got any choice," Claire said. "Anyway, you don't have to look cool all the time."

"I do, don't I?" Jason looked thoroughly miserable now. "And where's Philip?"

"I think he's chatting up that girl."

"Should be a laugh."

Claire giggled.

"He's probably explaining his theory of art to her."

She giggled again.

To have this effect on her, an actual physical, observable effect –

"Look, I'm getting out of here. I need some fresh air," Jason said. "Help me out, will you?"

Claire got up and moved Philip's chair.

"I'll come with you," she said.

"OK."

Debbie, Helen's friend, was left on her own. The English people had started talking to her, but they were dull as fuck, and she couldn't be arsed with it. She went over to another table, where Spiggsy was sitting. She knew him vaguely through his ex-girlfriend, a bitch called Louise. Soon they were dancing to some Bette Midler song Val was trying.

Spiggsy slid his hands down to her arse fairly quickly, thank fuck. Debbie had felt like a spare prick when Helen went off.

An old man was talking to the arts people.

"See them," he said, nodding at Debbie and Spiggsy. He chuckled, then leaned over to tap Dee-Dee's arm. "If you had a little kiss, when I was their age, you thought you were quite the laddie."

Dee-Dee laughed. "It's a different world, isn't it?"

"Now you see, I left school at thirteen, to go to work in the pit." He looked at Kelvin.

"We didn't have no helmets in them days, just our caps."

The phrase 'oral history' flashed on and off in the minds of all three arts people.

"It must have been hard back then," Dee-Dee said.

The old man chuckled. "Aye, a lot harder than it is now." He grinned and touched Dee-Dee's knee. "I used to love a little shag in them days," he said, and laughed until he coughed.

Jason and Claire left the pub behind and were heading for the darkness at the end of the road. There were seven pairs of streetlights ahead of them, then nothing.

Pink Floyd drifted out from a house they passed. Claire glanced in; the room was lit by a red bulb, and a magic carpet of pot-smoke hovered just below it.

Jason was silent. Claire hummed under her breath. They passed a pair of street lights. Somewhere a car revved up.

Claire cleared her throat, then went back to humming.

They passed another pair of streetlights. Then, Jason hurt his hand.

"Shit."

"What is it?"

"Grazed my palm on the wheelrim."

"OK?" Claire said.

"Yeah."

"You should get gloves. Leather ones."

"Maybe."

"Don't your arms get tired?"

"You get used to it."

"I can't get over how big they are."

Jason arched an eyebrow. There were three pairs of streetlights left.

"My arms?" he said.

"Yeah, they're massive. Roll your sleeves up."

"Don't take the piss, Claire."

"No, I mean it. Roll them up."

Another pair of lights went by. Only a few houses were left. There was no doubt where they were heading. Jason rolled up his sleeves.

"Bloody hell, look at the muscles on you," Claire said.

She winced. It sounded false and stilted. But it was working. However corny her lines were, they were moving the scene on. Claire circled her own left biceps with her right hand.

"I bet I couldn't do that with your arm," she said.

Jason glanced ahead, past the last two lights to where the mountain began. He gave a tiny nod, like a twitch, then turned back to Claire.

"Ah, I reckon you could," he said, holding out his arm. These words, these fucking bastard words. Stupid, corny, graceless crap. No choice, no choice. Shut up then.

They passed the last two lights. When the orange glow faded, Jason stopped and put on his brakes. There was nothing on either side of them now, just cool air. In the darkness, Claire moved towards Jason.

Philip and Helen were heading back down towards Treorchy.

"So, what do you do?" Philip asked.

"Make Christmas trees," Helen said. She sniggered. "I do, honest."

"I believe you."

"Whenever people ask me what I do, they never believe me."

"Well, y'know," Philip said. "I suppose somebody's got to do it, like."

A thin, high breeze whirred up the street. Philip shivered.

"I don't like it there though," Helen said.

"What, in the Christmas tree factory?"

"Yeah. It's boring."

"So, what would you –?"

"Hair and beauty," Helen said. "They do these courses in Llwynypia college. I'm thinking of doing one, because I know a lot about it, like."

"Yeah, I can tell."

Helen laughed. "Oh yeah?"

"Yeah, you look really good."

She was looking at him. "Try to be more specific."

"It's like," he began. "Yeah, it's like, most girls you see, well they look OK, but they don't sort of..."

She still hadn't looked away.

"I mean, you've got a kind of," he said. "A style. Yeah, y'know, everything you're wearing fits in, like, and your make-up and hair – it's like all part of your own style, y'know, individual like. And it looks really good, y'know, it makes you stand out from the crowd, from other girls, I mean."

Philip breathed.

"Are you winding me up?" Helen grinned.

"No, I mean it." Philip looked her straight in the eyes, and she knew he really did mean it.

"That's really nice," Helen said, "and it's weird, because that's exactly what I do, try to do anyway. You're really sweet, you know."

Philip did a cute little grin and looked away. They carried on walking, Philip shivering, Helen talking about hair-dye, running her fingers through Philip's black mop to illustrate various points.

"Hang on, I've got something in my shoe."

Helen grabbed Philip's shoulder for support and took her shoe off. Philip looked down. Her bra was decorated with lace flowers. She straightened up.

"Were you just looking at my tits?"

"I'm afraid so," Philip said.

"Did you like what you saw?"

"Well," Philip said, "yes I did."

"Want to see some more?"

He looked her in the eyes again.

"Yes, I do."

She took his hand – her hand was warm. She led him up a lane – the lane was dark. She pushed him against a garage door – he bumped his head. The skin across her shoulders was soft and firm, and he could feel her energy underneath. He pressed his palms against her, here and there, his fingers splayed. There was movement under her skin. There were pulses in unexpected places. He wanted to find out all about her, what was inside a girl.

Her tongue slid into his mouth. He tried to concentrate, but the insistence was starting now. She unzipped his jeans and he suddenly remembered Jason. He hoped Claire was keeping him company back at the pub. But then his heartbeat was pulsing through his cock, ticking away in her hand, and he forgot his friend, forgot his sister. He looked over her shoulder. A cat was slinking across a garden wall.

"Do you fancy me?" Helen whispered.

"Yeah." It came out in a breathy gasp. Nerves, probably. This was, after all, the first public appearance of his cock.

"Are you going to give it to me?" Helen said.

What an odd choice of words, like a porn mag caption. He turned his head to the side, embarrassed.

Suddenly he was spotlit. A car's headlights had turned the lane into the Albert Hall stage. Every stone cast a fifteen foot shadow. And, projected onto the white back wall of Supersave, Philip's cock, the length of a bus, twitched and bobbed. Its tip nudged a drainpipe. You could have seen it from Stuart Street.

Helen was shrieking, actually slapping herself with hilarity. The car got closer, and Philip's penis took one final bow, still in the spotlight, then hurried behind the curtain.

As they talked about other things, pretending not to notice, Claire's fingers traced patterns on Jason's upper arm. Claire told him she'd like to write an episode of *Eastenders*.

"You've got to take the story from point A to point B within that one episode," she said, "but stylistically, it's up to you how you do it."

Jason nodded, concentrating on the sensation of her index finger's nail reversing deliberately up his forearm.

"So you could do anything you liked then," he said.

"Yeah. You could do it all weird, like Ionesco," Claire said. "His plays were absurd," she explained.

"Were they," Jason said.

She started stroking his hair, talking all the time. His eyelids were heavy, Christ, he was practically purring. There was a vat inside him, full of something warm and sweet. It was seeping out, spreading through him.

"Philip is actually really clever though," she was saying. "He likes all that sort of stuff. He says we're all existentialists in the Rhondda."

What did she smell of? Coconut and fresh skin.

"He says coal was God, then he looks all intense and goes, 'But now God is dead'." She giggled.

Jason felt so sensitive he could detect the finest details. Her long hair was flowing past him, some resting on his shoulder. Concentrating, he could feel the few strands that had slipped inside his shirt and were lying on his bare skin. Everything in him stood on end.

"'God is dead and we are alone in this absurd valley'," Claire said, doing Phil's voice.

She made her final move. She was two inches from his face, her weight pressing on him. He felt a painful stabbing near his heart – the screw-cap of his hip flask digging into him. She moved closer. Her breathing was beautiful. Fourteen years old. Christ. She aimed at his lips, slid her arms fully around his neck.

He could die now, that would be fine. She kissed him. The back panel fell off the shoddy old world, and outside was something better. She slid the last few inches and he was cradling her on his lap, in his wheelchair, on a piece of waste-ground, a quarter of a mile from the pub. Thank fuck the brakes were on.

Step by step, scene building on scene, line on line; dramatic development – conclusion, denouement, climax, curtain. You could do anything you wanted, get anything you wanted. But Claire had done enough now. It was time to leave it to him. He could direct himself now. She stretched and curled in his arms. Yes, she'd done enough. She sighed against his neck. Yes.

If it wasn't for Helen squeezing his crotch in the car, Philip would have fucked off straight away. Spiggsy and Debbie, themselves looking for a likely place for a shag, had found Philip's giant erection instead. Now they were all going for a drink. It was going to be bad, but Philip had got single-minded.

It was time to get rid of his virginity. It didn't fit with his new image anyway. He'd toyed with the idea of an ambiguous anti-sexuality, but it was difficult to get the nuances across in Treorchy. Anyway, he had the biggest one in the world, as far as Debbie and Spiggsy were concerned. So they drove around to Treorchy.

Spiggsy wasn't drinking, but he was determined to get a bit shit-faced before the night was out. So he offered his wrap of speed around the car. Helen and Debbie got all blasé as they took some. They all sat in the car for a few minutes, the four of them, because Helen's favourite song had come on the radio.

"Pump up the jam," she sang.

"Pump pump pump pump pump up the jam," Debbie added.

Spiggsy drummed on the dashboard. It started to rain. Streetlights blurred as the windscreen became opaque. Cars went by, speeding up to get past the traffic lights before they changed.

It would look so crap if he didn't take the speed, now that it was being offered. Basically, schematically, it was like this: he couldn't be part of Minty's gang, he didn't want to be a 9 to 5er, and Nussbaum's lot were rancid. So that only left the disaffected underclass intellectual. And he couldn't do that without getting stuck in. For real.

Pattering on the roof, water streamed down. Treorchy was slowly turning into a smear. Coloured brightness on a black background. It was a night off, a break from trying to find his niche. Tonight, he'd crawl into someone else's. He took the speed. The song ended, they got out of the car and trooped into The Blacksmith.

Minty was in the pub. Obviously. Up by the pool tables. Wearing one of those shirts that looked like a Kentucky Fried

Chicken carton. Robert Palmer droned away on the jukebox, *Addicted to Love*, a song which always made Philip think of prolonged constipation. He went up and put on some techno stuff he wouldn't normally have touched with a shitty stick. Now he got off on the frantic clicking rhythms.

So this was what all that was about, raves. Obvious, really. It went – chukka chukka chukka chukka-kish, chukka chukka chukka kish. Then there were the fills, which went tiss-chakka, tiss-chakka, tiss-chakka. And he could do the sounds with his mouth, keeping the beat steady with his feet.

"We nearly pissed ourselves, didn't we?" Helen said.

Debbie nearly pissed herself there and then. Spiggsy was laughing too. Some freak of a shit-faced wank-pig was laughing, right in Philip's face, and you could see his sweat.

"What?"

Oh yeah, this was about his giant cock. To be fair, it was an amusing thing, *per se*. He laughed back. It was someone he'd been to school with, in fact, this wanking shit-pig.

"So, how's it going then?" Philip said, grinning.

"Blah blah blah something something blah blah something about party poppers, blah blah blah something about coppers something something mad laugh," the boy said.

Philip remembered the time they were in the gym, because it was raining, so they were doing touch rugby, and this boy had put his watch, a new one, digital, with a calculator on it, on top of the vaulting horse for safe keeping, and he, Philip, had accidentally nudged the horse, the vaulting horse, and the watch had fallen down the back, and it was really difficult to get to it as a result of it, the vaulting horse, being very tight against the wall, and there were some javelins there as well. So the boy, this boy here now, had got a bit upset, and Philip hadn't been as sympathetic as he might have been, then Mr Llewellyn came over and made this boy embarrassed by doing a stupid voice and saying stuff about him losing his watch, and was his mother going to give him a row, and moving the vaulting horse with one hand and scratching his curly hair with the other. Because Mr Llewellyn looked like Welsh men were supposed to. He was only about eighteen inches high, in fact, but he was twelve foot wide and had a dirty face all the time and one of those moustaches. And then he realised that he'd been saying all this out loud, and that people were laughing at him. It, therefore, needed a flourish.

"And that's how I got the idea for sump oil," Philip said, making a wide gesture to engulf the whole pub.

"Fucking mad," the boy said.

"Sump oil," Spiggsy laughed.

"Oi, what's that?" Helen said.

"What?" someone else asked.

"Sump oil," Debbie said.

"Sump oil?" the boy said.

Everyone looked at Philip who shrugged. He'd lost it.

"It's what you get in the sump," Spiggsy said.

"What's the sump?" someone asked.

And the music, funnily enough, went sump-sump-sump-sump OIL, sump-sump-sump-sump OIL. Well, no it didn't actually. It was all in the perception anyway. Like everything. Perhaps his penis really was fifteen feet long. Who was really to say?

A quick detour into the toilets, and fuck me if it wasn't jolly old Minty having a Jimmy Riddle. Don't look down. He'll think I'm Joe Orton. But he did look down, and all the piss was gathering around the drain hole of the trough, which was blocked up with fag ends, the colour of sump oil. Minty did his special look at Philip on the way out, the contempt, for no reason, just that look, like he owned a hundred shares in Philip but would rather sell them on.

"Can you not even –" Philip began.

Minty stopped in the doorway and turned.

"You know, even deign to speak to me," Philip said.

Minty was across the room and had Philip against the wall. But now he was here he looked a bit uncertain, like he'd forgotten his lines. Philip tried to help him.

"You know, I mean –"

"You fucking prick," Minty snarled, and one of his gums seemed to be bleeding a bit.

Then he shoved Philip away from him, against the wall.

Debbie, Helen and Spiggsy were getting their stuff together, along with his old schoolfriend. They all went out, got in the car and headed up the valley. He didn't know where they were going, but the ride was fun.

Metal over the windows.

"The council haven't come to take them off yet."

The front door was held on with string. Inside. Mould and someone else's letters. It was chitter-chatter cold. You went frrrrrrth and shivered.

Philip followed them all into the living room. A dark haired girl was sitting in an armchair. She wore black jeans and a small ankh around her neck. Debbie went over to the girl and put her arms around her shoulders. Her day-glo dress looked weird against the girl's black T-shirt.

"Hello love, can we stay for five?" Debbie said.

The girl nodded, her face blank as a fag packet.

"All right, Emma?" Helen said.

Another nod.

"Oh, I tell you what, I'm like an asshole," Helen said, putting her Grolsch bottle down.

There was a huge Iggy Pop poster over the mantelpiece. Philip leaned against it, and breathed deeply.

"This is Philip, by the way," Helen told the girl.

She looked at him and nodded. Perhaps she didn't even nod. Perhaps she didn't even look at him.

"Oh, I nearly pissed myself tonight," Helen said. "Didn't we, Deb?"

Debbie and Spiggsy started laughing, and Philip grinned. A puke might well be on the cards, in fact. Seeing that they were all relaxing, Philip slumped to the floor and let the wall keep his back straight. Helen told Emma the story, and Philip watched Emma. She smiled faintly at the story's punchline, but there was contempt in her eyes. Then Spiggsy went to light up a spliff and she suddenly came alive.

"If you want to do that, you do it outside," she said. Her voice was cold.

"Ah, come on Em, just a spliff," Spiggsy said.

"I don't give a fuck, you don't do it in here."

"We're all stoned anyway," he said.

"I've told you: you don't bring anything in here. You want to do it, fine – fuck off out."

Slowly, Spiggsy put the spliff down. He looked pissed off

"No, come on Spiggs, it's her flat, she don't want to have the coppers round, does she," Debbie said.

She went over and stuck her tongue in his mouth and he cheered up a bit. Emma got up and went to a cupboard. She took out a bottle of vodka, then walked over to a CD player. Music started happening.

"Oh, not this again," Helen said, but she was smiling. Insincere.

"Is this –?" Philip said. "Yeah, it's early Bowie, isn't it? His Anthony Newley phase."

Emma nodded.

"Has this got *Love You Till Tuesday* on it?" Philip asked.

He wasn't quite sure where in the valley they were. On some estate or other.

"Yeah," Emma said.

Helen seemed to suddenly notice that Philip and Emma were both dressed in black. She looked back at Spiggsy and Debbie, necking away on the armchair, then there was a little bit of talking and then she led him into a bedroom with a curtain held on by drawing pins. The last he saw of Emma was her drinking from the vodka bottle.

Helen fell asleep at around four thirty. He'd fucked her twice, but it was all a blur. She'd pulled, then tugged, and finally sucked, then it started to hurt and get big. She got on top. That was it. Twice. Philip was wide awake now, and cold. He slid his jeans and boots on and went to find the toilet. In the bathroom his breath steamed out in front of him. He couldn't think of anything except how cold he was. His jaw ached from chattering away, doing the cold talk: tutta tutta tutta frrr-rrrr-eeee-zzing brr-brr-brr t-t-t-t-t, all the fucking time. The walls seemed to be in a cold sweat. His arms looked like winter branches. He had to get some heat.

The coal fire in the living room. He had to try it. He

staggered in through the door and warmth drew huge shivers through his flesh. It was dark. Spiggsy and Debbie had gone. The room slowly pulsed orange. He moved towards the fire. It was hidden by an armchair with a lumpy quilt on it. He moved closer. Two brown eyes gazed up at him from the chair. Emma was curled up in it, looking at him, upside down.

"I was cold," he said, shivering. "Cold."

He was sagging on the tail-end of the speed as it ran out. Emma held open the quilt, letting out her heat. It flowed towards him. He closed his eyes, swayed on his feet. That's what he needed. Heat. He folded, bit by bit, like a slow motion demolition. It was warm inside Emma's quilt.

The morning, then. Some glue had stopped up his eyes, so he just listened to the hammering on the door, then felt Emma detach herself and get up. The cold hissed in where her body had been. Philip shivered. A voice was ranting on somewhere in the flat. It sounded heavy. Someone was in for a kicking. His eyes ripped open. A kicking. Shit. He started hunting for his trousers.

"I know he's in here," the voice said.

Emma said something, but he couldn't make it out.

"Look, I don't want to cause trouble, but I'll knock the fucking door down unless –"

Philip jumped into his jeans, pulling on a boot. Where the fuck was the other one? He could always jump out the window if he had to. No, they had metal on them. Where the fuck was he anyway? He was sure they hadn't left the valley last night. Then he heard Spiggsy's voice, loud and defensive. The two male voices were arguing. It didn't seem to be his fight, thank fuck. He peered around the living room door.

"I don't give a fuck, you better come out here now and we'll sort it out."

It was some bloke, one of Minty's mates.

"All right, fucking hell, let me get my shoes on, fuck's sake," Spiggsy said, but he looked scared.

Helen and Debbie poked their heads around the door, mouthing things to each other. Spiggsy came out of the bedroom, fully dressed. Minty's mate started hurrying him.

"All right, fuck off, I'm coming, ain't I?" Spiggsy said.

There was a bit of a scuffle. Craning his neck a bit further he could see Emma standing there, looking monumentally bored. And beyond that, through the front door, a red Escort. XR3i. Fuck it. Minty.

With a push the back door opened and he stumbled through. A frantic rush through the brambles in the garden and he reached a fence, clambered over and fell down a grassy verge. He stopped himself just in time. Didn't fall off the wall. He got on to the road and set off down. When he was past the next set of houses he looked around. He was in Treherbert, about three miles from home. More specifically he had spent a night on The Ranch, where they said the syringes were ankle-deep in the playground. It looked nice enough, but he was too fucked to tell, really.

Philip called in Spar and bought a pint of milk, then walked back down to Treorchy. All the way back nothing went through his mind, nothing in words anyway. He tried to think about that, but it just slipped back to a buzz. He was like a television after closedown. People were on their way to work, but he hardly saw them looking at him from their cars and buses.

He was near the top of his street when he looked at his watch. It was eight thirty. Thursday morning. That made it even stranger, then, to see Jason and Claire like that, just strolling along The Boulevard, where normally at this time it would just be old men taking their dogs for a morning shit. But he just hurried across the road, let himself into the house and went straight upstairs to bed.

Hours later, when there were afternoon noises coming through the window, he woke up and saw Jason on the mattress, fast asleep. His friend murmured a few times, said "more", and grinned, before turning on his side. Philip went to the toilet for a piss. His penis looked different. Fatter, more substantial somehow. Jason was right – more.

8. JUNE 1993.

Through the window Jason watched them drive off, his father's Escort and his mother's Volvo. They reached the end of the street and one turned right, the other left. He relaxed and turned to look at the flat. It was a nice one, and you hardly noticed the modifications – the widened doors, the handles here and there, like in the bog. Three floors up, a lift that always worked and security lock doors in the lobby. And the rent was covered by his benefits. All he'd done to swing it was convince Martin Greaves that he'd visit the group regularly. Piece of piss.

He wheeled over to the phone, dodging his cardboard boxes. He dialled the McKays' number and Philip answered.

"Phil, this is a call from the Morgan residence."

"You're in?"

"Yup. This morning."

"Are you on your own?"

"Yeah. They just left. Didn't want to, but I convinced them."

"What's it like then? Groovy?"

"Very much so. Find out for yourself. Coming down? Flat-warming?"

"Ah, well, it's a bit tricky tonight."

"What? Why?"

"Well, I've sort of got a date."

"Again? The same one?"

"No, no. Another one."

"Aren't you ever satisfied?"

"Not so far, no."

"You randy old bastard."

"The funny thing is, though, it's not so much the shtupping itself..."

"Bullshit."

"No, seriously. It's the, kind of, the nerve of it. Know what I mean?"

109

"I know they always seem to be engaged to someone or other."

"Yeah, exactly. They're always going out with someone who'd rip my lungs out if they knew. Hard lads, you know, the type who look at me and you as if we're shit." He giggled then sighed.

"Nice hobby, Phil," Jason said.

"Oh, fuck off, Jase. We're the No-Hope Twins, aren't we?"

"Yeah, whatever. So you're not coming down?"

"Sorry mate. Tomorrow?"

"That's cool."

There was silence for a few seconds.

"Do you want to talk to Claire?" Philip said.

Jason scratched his head.

"Is she there?"

"Yeah. I don't think she's doing anything tonight."

"Are you OK about this?" Jason asked.

"Yeah, fine. She's smart enough to, well, you know, to know what she's doing. That's what everyone says."

"Look, Phil, it's not like it's, you know," Jason said. "I mean, she's fifteen for God's sake."

"Yeah, I know, I know."

"I mean, we just talk, you know."

"Jase, shut up, I'm not asking, just leave it. I'll put her on."

"Thanks Phil."

"It's OK, it's cool."

"Have a good one tonight."

"I'll try."

"But look, be fucking careful, right? I'm serious. I'd feel like it was my fault if anything..."

"Your fault?"

"I know. Stupid, isn't it?"

"Nothing's going to happen. It's all about being fast."

"Yeah, in and out before they notice."

"That's right. Look, here's Claire. Call me tomorrow. But not in the morning."

"OK, cheers mate."

"Where you off tonight then, son?" Val said.

"Down The Bridge," Philip said.

"Ah, there's entertainment in The Bridge, isn't there?"

"There's a band on tonight. Pigswill, they're called."

"Check them out for me, will you?"

"What for?"

"You've got to keep up with the competition."

"Dad, I don't think you and Pigswill are fighting over the same patch, really. Besides, I thought you were happy just doing the Lion?"

"I might branch out, you know. Bring my music to more people, spread a bit of the joy around." He chuckled.

Claire came through from the dining room.

"OK if I stay down Catherine's tonight?" she said, airily gathering up some of her folders from the armchair. She cast a quick glance at Philip as Val made a joke about wild teenage parties.

Upstairs, in his room, Philip put his boots on, ready to go out. Claire said "knock-knock" and came in.

"Going out?" she said.

"Yeah, going to see a band in The Bridge."

"You should stay in and do some writing. This theatre project is getting nowhere. You've been stalling for months."

"Claire, I've got other things on my mind."

"I know what they are. Just get on with it. Please. For me."

"Anyway, I don't know if it's such a good idea. Having Jason in it, I mean."

Her eyes narrowed. "What do you mean?"

"I don't think he really wants to be in it."

"He didn't at first, no. But I've talked to him, and he's quite looking forward to it now."

Philip sighed. "It's Kelvin and those clowns..."

"It's not about them. It's about me. And Jason. And you, if you ever write the bloody scripts."

"Whatever, whatever. I'm going out." He stood up and put his jacket on. "And so are you."

"Walk me to the station?"

"Yeah, OK."

What really surprised Philip was how easy it was to fuck someone. The secret was not to be afraid to ask. A lot of girls said yes. He realised they had a lot of different reasons. Some wanted to get back at their boyfriends. Some wanted to get back at their families. Some couldn't get off very easily and kept trying different people. So many reasons made good odds.

Like this one here, Laura. He watched her, and himself, in the mirror on the far wall. She was drinking from her bottle of lager, swaying to the music. And there he was, Philip, pretending not to be with her, just in case. Her boyfriend, it seemed, wouldn't touch her when she was on. He had a thing about it. Philip knew him vaguely. Corky. Quite a hard bastard. On the fringes of Minty's coterie. On the payroll, probably, somewhere along the line. And yet he had this squeamish side. Which was bad for Laura, as she felt most randy when she was on.

All this she'd told Philip one day, completely out of the blue. This was where he could beat them, the hard lads: in the listening. Getting them to talk to him. They couldn't do it, just grunted a lot and posed. But to him, they'd talk. He knew just what to say. From there it was incredibly easy. The tricky bit was not getting caught. The girls always knew it was a one-off, so they wouldn't say anything. It was up to him to be a bit fly.

This was what kept him doing it. That he could beat them, by using his brains, without them even knowing. He could walk down the street these days with his head held high, even if they spat at his big clumpy boots. That fucking niche never came along, all that happened was you stuck out like a sore thumb, more and more, and every fucker would kick your head in if they could even be bothered. He knew it was ridiculous, of course it was, but then everything was, so what the fuck?

Pigswill were hammering through '*Pretty Vacant*', the toilet walls vibrating with the bass, and Philip fucked Laura to the beat – thump-uh, thump-uh, thump-uh. In the bogs, in The Bridge, with the boys outside posing, so hard uh-yeah, her sweaty little body twisting as he tried to hold her steady.

112

Almost singing along, gasping. *You'll always find me out to lunch*; and whenever he lost his nerve he just thought for a second about what he was doing, pictured it, in detail, and powered on, eyes wide open. We're so pretty, oh so pretty, we're vay-cunt. Before the song was over he pulled it out and came like a fountain, over the cistern. Then they had a wet kiss, tasting each other's sweat, and grinned at each other, their eyebrows pointing down, before sneaking out and away separately; and that was their date.

It was still quite early when he got home, just gone midnight. He put a Tom Waits CD on and lit a fag. Looking around the room at all the books, the videos, the CDs, Philip felt pretty good about himself. This was the niche, wasn't it? He was well-read, imaginative, his best friend was a vengeful alcoholic paraplegic who was in love with his kid sister, he had an exciting sex life – well, more than that, it was kind of significant, wasn't it? It said something, made some kind of statement. If someone in the future wrote his biography, the nineteen year old Philip would make pretty good reading.

He walked along the landing to Claire's room and picked up her lap-top word processor. They wouldn't, of course, write his biography unless he did something. So that had to be the next stage – writing something. He put the word processor on his desk, stuck the fag in the corner of his mouth, and got to work.

9. July 1993.

It took Jason fifteen minutes to get the leather trousers on. Claire was busy setting the scene up, her ponytail bobbing up and down as she marched across the stage with her clipboard.

"Right, so we've got," she paused, looked confused, flipped over a few pages of her notes, nodded.

"Yeah, we've got Giro George, the Speed Lizards, The Tart with a Heart and then the narrative. Ben, how's that going?"

Ben Wilmott scratched his head. "OK, I suppose. I'm not sure about this bit, I think you've left the punctuation out. Page thirty-one."

Claire looked at her script. "No, that's right as it is. I think. Philip wrote it." She peered out into the audience. "Hey, Phil."

He looked up from his notepad, his hair a terrible mess. "What?" he shouted.

"Page thirty-one," Claire called. "Ben's narrative. It's supposed to be like that, is it?"

"Like what?" Philip roared.

Claire turned to Ben. "Yeah, that's right as it is."

"OK, whatever," Ben muttered.

"Hey, Phil," Claire shouted.

"What?"

"We're doing Jason's bit in about two minutes."

"Nearly finished," Philip shouted and went back to chewing his pen.

"OK Ben," Claire said, "just give me the last bit of the narrative."

Ben shrugged and looked at the script. "We take fragmentation for granted split the seams and all the shit comes out a hundred varieties of nothing used up all available energy no more returns time to be numb entropy vending pack railway track." He stopped to breathe. "Why is there something instead of nothing we're so cold don't you love us anymore Little Moscow cynical actors this game is crooked extended adolescence now wash your hands."

"Yeah, nice," Claire said, and rushed across the stage into the wings.

Philip grinned at Ben, who shrugged and went through the lines again, trying to work out where to breathe.

Backstage, Jason guiltily put his hip-flask away in mid-swig when he saw Claire.

"I didn't know this was a bloody dress rehearsal, Claire."

"It's not, I just wanted to see how you'd look," Claire said.

"So it's just me dressed up then, is it?"

Jason was dressed from head to foot in black leather, with dented metal pads strapped on here and there. Wraparound shades stuck out of a pocket, the replica shotgun over his knees. Claire looked him over, came closer, smiled.

"So, how do I look?" Jason said, frowning.

"Pretty sexy, actually," she said, running her hand over him. "Now let me spike your hair up and we'll be ready."

She started running gel through his hair. Jason sat in his wheelchair, not thinking of anything in particular. He felt just right. He had the girl, he had the moves. Like some film, with a hard embittered bastard, fucked up but sexy, and he was going to tell them all a few bastard home truths. He felt – suave.

"I think they'll be needing the script soon," Kelvin said.

"Right, right, I've done it, there, finished, see?" Philip underlined what he'd written and jumped up from his seat. He was about to climb on the stage when Claire emerged from the wings.

"OK, ladies and gentlemen, here he is," she said.

Philip looked up as Jason wheeled onto the stage, following Claire out to the centre.

"Doesn't he look great?" Claire said.

Philip's mouth fell open and he backed away, bumping against Kelvin's seat.

"He does, doesn't he?" Kelvin said.

Philip's eyes widened. "Oh God, he looks like an arsehole."

Kelvin looked puzzled.

"He looks like an early prototype for the Terminator," Philip said.

Seeing that Kelvin was still confused, Philip leaned over the seat towards him.

"He looks like Schwarzeneger would if he did his own stunts. He looks like a nancy boy. He looks like a fucking monkey."

"Well I hardly think – " Kelvin began.

"Philip – script," Claire said, reaching down.

Her brother looked up at her, towering over him on the stage, her hand grasping the air. Slowly he handed over his notepad, staring at her.

"What's the matter with you?" she hissed.

"I hope you know what the fuck you're doing," Philip whispered.

Claire grinned. "I'm doing a performance," she told him and took the script.

"Fucking right," Philip muttered, turning his back on the stage.

"Is this thing loaded?" Jason asked, pointing his gun at Ben Wilmott, who flinched.

"No, but there'll be blanks in it on the night. For now, just go 'bang'."

She waltzed across the stage, sweeping people away from Jason's space.

"Right, music swells, spots on, cue Jason," she said, skipping away stage right.

Jason brushed some fag ash off Phil's notepad and started his speech.

"They call me The Crawler, or The Abortion. The less imaginative ones call me Spastic. They only call me these names once."

He cocked his shotgun, swung it into his right hand.

"I'm The Cripple: smashed legs, fucked spine, dumb cells, loaded shotgun. I'm in your town. I'm not going away. A cripple with a gun – your worst nightmare. Your neighbourhood is full of fuckers and junkies, wankers and pricks, bigots and bastards, speed vendors and their groupies, bent cops, magistrates, masons, schoolgirl whores, sugar daddies with gold chains, full-backs and fly-halves, commuters and porn freaks, girls with Ford Fiestas and menstrual cramps, boys who

116

crave snooker and anal sex, fascist shop stewards and men who'd give their own lungs to fuck their daughters."

Jason swung the shotgun up, aimed at the audience and pulled the trigger.

"BANG!" he shouted.

Philip slumped in his seat.

"Ohh... God." He put his hand over his eyes.

Jason swung the gun back to his side.

"Crippled, twisted, crushed, you wiped me off your boots. From down there I saw you all, doing your endless sick dance. I wrapped my rattling bones in leather, dragged myself up through your filth, and now we need to talk. A cripple with a grudge – your worst nightmare."

He pointed the gun at the audience again. Philip was looking down the barrel. Jason shouted bang.

"If you told the truth for just one day, one hour, a minute, you'd give yourselves – oh – FUCK SHIT PISS BOLLAAAAAAAAAAAAAAACKS!"

He flung the gun and the notepad out into the audience, where they clattered down behind Philip and Kelvin. Philip hid even further, sliding off the seat altogether.

"Philip!" Jason shouted. "Oi, Philip! I know you're down there, don't try and fucking hide!"

Claire came rushing across to Jason, but he thrust out a black gloved finger at her.

"Wait," he growled. She froze.

"Philip, come on, come out, you little bastard."

His tousled black hair appeared, followed by his pale face.

"Yeah?"

"What the fuck do you think you're doing?" Jason shouted.

"Nothing," Philip said.

"Don't piss me about, what's this fucking shit you're making me say? It's the biggest load of bollocks I've ever heard in my life."

"Well, look, I tried to –"

"I don't give a hairy fuck. I've had enough of your shit, you poncey bastard."

"Jase, come on, I never said I was –"

Kelvin seemed about to say something, then sat back, watching closely.

"Don't give me that crap, you bullshitter. What's all this 'fuck their daughters' shit? What's that supposed to mean? And what the fuck's it got to do with me? You've got your head up your arse."

He let his brakes off and came to the front of the stage.

"You're making me look a prick, you two-faced bastard."

Philip stood up, knocking over Kelvin's coffee cup, and turned away down the aisle, saying something as he went.

"What did you say?" Jason roared.

"It's not me," Philip shouted, "that's making you look a prick."

He walked off along the aisle.

Kelvin decided it was time to impose a little adult authority on things.

"OK, well obviously we need to take five, perhaps go away and re-evaluate a few things. But the important thing is the amount of energy, of power, that this play is generating. I think you're all doing very well."

It took Jason fifteen seconds to get the leather trousers off. He flung them across the dressing room and started putting his jeans on. There was a knock on the door.

"Fuck off Claire," he yelled.

"Can I come in?" he heard her say.

"No, you can fuck off." He struggled out of the leather jacket and wheeled over to fetch his own jacket.

Claire peered around the door.

"Look, don't go yet. I'll..."

"I said fuck off," Jason shouted, wheeling across the room. Claire opened the door and he shot through. She chased him down the corridor.

"Jason," she said, "wait, I've had an idea — you write your own words. Yeah?"

"Claire, just fuck off and leave me alone."

"No, Jason, don't go."

He stopped at the side door.

"Why not?"

"I need you," Claire said.

"Tough shit."

"Jason..."

"Find some other fucker."

He hurried back to the McKays' house, hoping nobody was in. He would pick up his stuff and fuck off. He went along the lane, past ducks qua-qua-quacking and a kid with a bleeding knee shouting for his friends.

"Boys! Boys! Wait there! Boys!"

When he got to the top of the lane four oily lads were gathered around a car, pissing with the engine. An old man with a dog came around the corner, looked away from the boys but smiled cheerily at Jason. The boys, without taking their hands out of the engine, glanced at him, their noses wrinkling, lips curling.

He wheeled along The Boulevard, avoiding the turds, reaching out to scrape his knuckles on the long grey river wall. Somewhere a car with a fucked exhaust revved up, and a dog barked.

"Boys! Boys! Hang on! Boys!"

He parked his chair on the bridge, looking down their street, and took out the hip-flask.

He just needed a couple of minutes. Over his head the sky went, grey, a high blank ceiling, the mountains flat like hoardings. His eyelids drooping, he slipped into neutral, fixing on the hip-flask, his gold initials, J.M., blurring to shiny fuzz. His stomach felt half-full of warm gravel.

This was... what was it? Wednesday?

A little black dog came along, pissed on his wheels and scurried off. Looking down through the metal grid he saw the river, fifteen feet below him. After the flood, God wised up and said he'd never bring shit down on the earth again, because he'd realised man was evil in his heart, from his youth up. So Satan was redundant, just God watching everything all the time.

But there were pockets, between the bottle bank and the paper bank in the car park, or holed up in his flat, in pockets

119

of booze, on this bridge, hidden by all this nature, plants sprouting and waving around; pockets.

At dusk, two months back; on top of a car-park in Cardiff, with Claire, looking out over the city as it turned into a jewellery box. And later, in his new flat, kissing her again, touching her, among his un-packed boxes. She would go on, but Jason stopped it every time. Just in time. He didn't want to be clambering around like a fucking great ape. Oh God, oh bollocks. He paused it before it could get awful. He had to keep that little pocket, where the shit didn't come down on him. It had to be like that. Claire, with her green eyes narrowing, computer on-line indicators, weighing it all up. Fifteen.

She'd use him up, take whatever bit of energy he had, move on. He was Claire's. He was really in trouble now. He fell asleep until a passing train shook him.

"Looks like rain," Jon said, peering out.

"Yeah," Philip said, checking his watch.

Going on for five now. The road outside the cafe was jammed up with cars. People squeezed between brake lights, appearing and disappearing like pantomime villains through the exhaust smoke.

"Going out tonight?" Jon asked from behind the counter.

Philip sighed. "Well, that's the question, isn't it? Go out or stay in?"

The lights were on in the theatre. Claire would still be in there. Jason too, probably.

Whatever was going on between them, whatever, Jason would stay. Like earlier – blaming Philip when it was her fault for getting them into all this. Claire believed her own publicity, that was it. Everyone saying what a gifted child she'd been, what a mature girl. She wouldn't handle Jason. No way. Well, fuck 'em both.

"Give us another fiver's worth of change, Jon," said the old woman playing the fruit machine.

Philip bought some fags and left. He shivered in the wind. Not much of a summer. He leaned on the traffic lights watching the cars for a little while.

The niche, the biography, the significance – none of it seemed real suddenly. There was just nothing around. Everything went up its own arse – music, books, everything. It was plastered over colour supplements before it even kicked off. But he couldn't just go home, he wasn't in the mood for reading tonight. Something had to be done, whatever it was. And the only life around here, the only thing going on was in dodgy pubs and rented flats, the back seats of uninsured cars. Some girls went giggling past him. He sighed. They were making a criminal out of him, these people, he'd never get a job on Radio 4 at this rate. He grinned but a cold gust of wind turned it into a grimace. He walked away, looking for tonight's bit of heat.

Claire stood between two sets of mirrors, washing her face. The mirror routine was the oldest one in the book, but still one of the best. Behind and in front of you a bright corridor stretches off forever. Your own head and shoulders are repeated endlessly, regularly spaced and identical. All the resonances are there. She enjoyed being there, between the mirrors, where the metaphors hung in the air. It could be a journey through time, always inhabiting now but always moving. Or it could be her many different identities, all the different Claires. It could be anything she wanted it to be, but the main thing was it looked good, symbolic.

She washed her face and hands and dried herself with paper towels. She felt good now, fresh, and she started to put her eyeliner on. You could make your eyes seem bigger than they were. There was a technique. Jason always said things about her eyes, that they didn't fit her face. Everyone said that: they were too narrow, they looked cold; as though she were doing something wrong. When he said it, though, he meant it as a compliment. Jason did everything backwards. In his world, everything was reversed.

Jason. Jason, Jason, Jason – what should she do now? She could calm him down, perhaps even get him back into the play. But she had to think further than that. Think.

Get him off the bottle. Bloody Philip buying him that hip-flask for his birthday. She had to keep buying him vitamins, making sure he took them, one a day. And friends, he needed them too. A job. She was just coming up to sixteen, catching Jason up. It was like he wasn't growing up at all, him or Philip. She would catch up with Jason in just a few years now.

They would go everywhere together then, the two of them. Everybody would know them. She had university to look forward to, all the contacts she could make, and Jason would be there, by her side, and all the people would know and remember them. And he was so handsome too, so sexy, looking up at her with his dark eyes, his big, tense shoulders. The way he held her, like he'd die if he let go, fall off a cliff, drown in the sea. The way he touched her.

Leaning on the sink, looking into her green eyes, Claire saw the eyeliner wasn't working. They were so narrow now. So what? It was just her body, that was all. She couldn't help it.

Jason was on the train travelling down the valley. He thought back to his surreal conversation with Val. He'd just got his stuff together and was about to leave, pissed off with the McKays and their home town, when Val came in. It was his last day at work, so he'd knocked off early and gone for a drink.

He invited Jason to share a glass of whisky with him.

"Yeah, I'll have one, thanks," Jason said.

Val opened the sideboard, took out his bottle of Bells and two glasses. He squinted into them.

"They're a bit dusty."

He poured the whisky, handed a glass to Jason and sat down at the dining table. Then he just talked for ages about why he was made redundant. The old bus company had been sold off and there were loads of new companies springing up.

"That's the end for the old red buses now, the old 54 seaters," he said. "Instead there'll be all colours of the rainbow. They showed us the tenders. You'll have Vale Travel, G.K. Buses, Glenfield Transport, Goldcrest Line, the Celtic Hoppers, Mini Shoppas, Bustlers, hustlers and bloody cattle rustlers as well, probably."

He and Jason laughed, taking big sips of Bells. Val shifted in his chair, resting his back on the wall. He fiddled with the Tesco bag on the table, the shape of his sandwich box emerging from the crackling folds.

"They're all these little eighteen seater things, supposed to come every three minutes, all competing with each other. You watch, it'll be like bloody Ben Hur out there on a Saturday morning. All up and down the valley, these multicoloured things cutting each other up to get to the bus queues first."

Jason raised his eyebrows. "Sounds like chaos."

"Chaos," Val agreed. "The valley roads will be red with blood by the end." He laughed bitterly. "And who's going to be doing the brakes on these things?"

"I don't know."

"I'll tell you: whichever bloody cowboy charges the least, that's who. They won't take on blokes like me, they've just got ordinary car mechanics doing it. I mean, I'm nothing special like, but I've worked on buses for twenty three years. Not just me, the others down at the depot too. A bus is a different animal to a car. They may seem the same but there's a lot of little differences, a lot of little mistakes you can make. Any of them mistakes can be fatal, especially if you're driving like a lunatic."

Val went on to ask him how the day felt when there was nothing to do. The question made him uncomfortable, from Phil's father. It was quiet in the dining room, and the afternoon was starting to get dark. Occasionally a car would pass through the street. They were sitting opposite each other, drinking.

So Jason said, "It's OK until about five in the afternoon. Then you start getting restless. See, you didn't get out of bed until two, so by five you're wide awake and want something to do. But everywhere is closing then, except pubs and off-licences. So you watch the news, then go and have a drink. You don't get up until two the next day, and about five you start to get restless. And that's that."

Val thanked Jason for cheering him up, and they both pissed themselves laughing. Then Jason excused himself, before either of Val's children got home.

"You're not waiting for Phil, then?" Val said.

"No, I've got to get back," Jason said. "I've got a few things to do."

"You're a good lad, Jason," Val said, opening the front door for him. "You want to leave off the booze a bit though. You'll get as fat as me."

They had a last laugh at that then Jason left.

Now he was on the train, hoping to catch the off-licence at the end of his street before it closed. There was a shouting charge behind him. He turned to see a group of boys storming through the closing doors and onto the train. Laughing, swearing, they piled into the end carriage, the eight-seater where Jason had to sit because of his wheelchair.

"Come on, boys, let's get in here."

"Fuck off, the guard goes through here."

"Fuck him. If he wants money he can suck my cock."

Jason sat still, looking at his hands, as they piled in. He barely noticed the very skinny one with the staring eyes until he vaulted right over the luggage rack, his boots just missing Jason's head. He jerked back in his chair.

"Shit!"

A head popped up over the seat-backs, shaved and stoned.

"Problem?" it said.

"No, I'm alright." Jason waved his hand dismissively.

The boy grabbed and shook it.

"Better get your nurse," he said, grinning.

Jason tried to get his hand back, but the boy pulled on it and made Jason stroke the side of his face.

"Boys!" he shouted. "He's trying to fuck me! Help, get him off me!"

His friends laughed and shook their heads, noted approvingly that he was a fucking nutter.

"Don't! Get off!" the boy screamed at Jason. "I might catch it!"

Jason's hand clenched, trying to make itself into a fist.

"No, no! I know you love me but you've got to let me go!" the boy shouted.

124

He let Jason's hand go then looked at the trembling cripple, who was gritting his teeth and staring back at him.

"Sorry about that, you poor fucking spastic," the boy said, his face a mask of concern. "You'll find some other fucker."

He grinned and disappeared behind the seats.

The train was moving on, down the valley, towards Jason's distant flat. He sat in his wheelchair, his jaw hurting from being so clenched. One of the boys got up and went to the sliding door of the end carriage. He slid it closed then kicked the handle three times. The door made an unhealthy noise.

"Boys, let's see the fucking guard get through that!"

In the back room of The Colliers with a crackly old Beatles song on the jukebox, Philip put his hand on Julie's leg.

"So where's the other half tonight then, eh?" he said.

"Fuck knows," Julie said, shaking her head. "I'm fucking sick of him. Sick of the sight of him. I told you he sold the telly, didn't I?"

"Yeah. What was it for again?"

"Oh, fuck knows. He'd owed some money to Minty, and Minty sent one of his mates around and Darren said not to let him in, so we were sitting there in the living room, watching a video and they kicked the front door in. I shit myself."

"I bet."

"They were going to beat the shit out of Darren but he gave them the telly instead. So he didn't even sell it really, just gave it to them."

"Right in the middle of your video." Philip smiled at her.

"Yeah, I know," Julie said, smiling back at him. "So he's out tonight, fuck knows where, he phoned to say he wouldn't be back until the day after tomorrow. And we were supposed to be going up the Seventh Heaven tonight."

"Anything I can do to help?" Philip pulled a suggestive face, and they both laughed.

Beer cans were flying around the carriage, clanging against the sides. They'd gone mad, fucking mad, all of a sudden. They were just rowdy bastards one minute, the next they exploded all over the carriage, like fucking baboons. Whatever they'd taken before they came out must have just kicked in. His chair was backed as far away from them as he could get it, which was about six feet. There were seven of them, and the one in the luggage rack was getting closer. Where was the fucking guard?

"Come here, sexy, give us a kiss!"

It was skinny boy again. He was right in Jason's face, leaning on his chair.

"Have you ever had a shag, my friend?" he hissed.

Oh shit, a genuine psycho.

"Do you wank? Uh-uh-uh-uh-uh!"

What the fuck was he doing?

"Look boys! Look at me! Look at me!"

He jumped on Jason's lap, one arm around his shoulder, punching the air with the other arm.

"Me and the spastic! Me and the spastic! Yeah!"

They were laughing, cheering him on. The guard, for God's sake, the guard, do your fucking job.

"Let's see what's in here then!"

Giggling, he reached down between his own legs and started on the button fly of Jason's 501's.

Jason smashed him, hard, on the side of the head. Skinny boy toppled over, his legs hooking on the chair, pulling it with him. Jason swung wildly but it was too late. The boy went over and took the chair with him. His boot flew up as he hit the floor, kicking Jason's head as he came tumbling after. He sprawled, trying to get upright, while Skinny Boy lashed out with another two kicks.

"You fucking spastic cunt, you fucking twat."

His face was completely exposed, the cocky bastard. So Jason gritted his teeth and punched him right in the mouth, hard.

"Fuck you!" Jason shouted.

The skinny boy grunted as he fell, and Jason felt his nose wrinkle up in a little grin, his teeth still bared. The boy was bleeding, stumbling around the carriage. Two of his friends had piled in and were kicking Jason as well, but they could only

126

get to his legs. He felt nothing as they stamped on his knees.
He just kept hammering at the door, shouting,

"Come on, you fucking bastards!"

Then he hit the release catch on his chair and one of the
metal arm rests fell into his hands. He swung it and smashed
one fucker in the chest, then took a stab at the other's head.

"Come on, then, motherfuckers!" Jason screamed, waving
the arm rest around.

The door suddenly opened and he fell through. Two guards
and some passengers piled in. The speeding boys were into it
and they trampled Jason to get stuck in. He crawled along the
dirty floor, trying to get clear. A man in a rugby shirt grabbed
his arms and pulled him away. There was a massive lurch as
the train came to a stop, then a jerk back. The fighters fell
about. The man dropped Jason on to a three-seater, and
plunged back into the fight, throwing someone around the
carriage. Then everyone fell about again as the train started up
and growled away. They were trampling his wheelchair.

Philip was in Seventh Heaven, a club on one of the roads out
of the valley. He'd gone along with Julie in the mini-bus, a
tangle of scruffy black hunched up against leggings, micro-
skirts and glistening thighs, jangling jewellery and perfume that
stuck in a lump at the back of his throat.

Now he was squeezed into a corner seat next to Julie and a
boy who kept scratching his forehead with one hand and
rolling two dice with the other.

"Want some of this?" Julie asked.

"I wouldn't say no," Philip leered.

"I meant this," Julie grinned, offering him a wrap of speed
under the table.

"Well, just a sprinkle. I wouldn't want my performance to
be affected."

"Your what?"

"My performance."

"Yeah...?"

"Wouldn't want it to be affected, like. It was a joke, you
know?"

"Don't take the piss, I know exactly what you mean."

"Yeah, sorry, it's a bit noisy, isn't it?"

"What?"

"I said, I've impetigo around the mouth of my anus."

Julie looked confused. "You've got what?"

"Genital warts," Philip said.

With a sweet smile he took the speed to the toilets. He helped himself to a tiny bit, just to keep him awake. He sat on the cistern for a minute, listening to branches hitting the window. It was a filthy night.

On his way back to the bar he bumped into Helen, his first fuck. Every time he saw her his mind flashed on Emma, that girl, that night, lying upside down on the armchair, two eyes peering out from the quilt, the coal fire, her warmth, sleeping with her, just sleeping, her whispering to him, half-asleep stuff, breathing out on to his neck, warm.

"Hey, Helen," he said.

She was crying, and looked up sadly.

"Hey, come on, come on, what's the matter?" Philip said.

"Fucking Kevin," she sobbed. "The bastard, that fucking bastard."

"Who's Kevin?"

"Kevin Selway," she said, slurring a bit. "You know him, he goes around with Cobbsy and all them."

"OK, Kevin, so what about him?"

"He's not fucking here, is he?"

"Where's he gone?"

"I don't fucking know." She belched, then sobbed again.

"Look, Hel, I think you'd better go home, you know, just chill out for a bit."

"I can't, can I?" Helen said. "I haven't got any money."

Some girls passed and Helen flinched.

"Bloody Pandy girls are after me too."

"Why?"

"Because I go around with Debbie, and they're after Debbie."

"Well, why are they after Debbie?"

"I don't know, do I? Something to do with a boy. Or a car. I don't know."

Philip went through his pockets and found a crumpled fiver.

"Look, get a taxi," he said. "It's still early."

She looked at the money, then wiped her eyes.

"You know Spiggsy and all them are after you?"

"Why?"

"You get on their tits. You and that one in the wheelchair. They think you're weird."

She took the fiver.

"Who else, besides Spiggsy?"

"Most of that lot. Kevin. Julie's boyfriend, Darren. Minty."

Philip put a fag in his mouth. "When you say they're after me…"

"Just don't piss them off, that's all."

"You've got to laugh, haven't you?" Philip said.

Helen smiled and turned to go.

"Hey, Helen, before you go, do you ever see Emma around?"

"Emma? No, she doesn't come out any more. Not at all. We sometimes go up her house, like. Mick's up here tonight."

"Who's Mick?"

"Her friend. He'll tell you about her."

The police car drove off into the murky night, its tail lights dissolving. Jason watched them go then went up the wheelchair ramp into his building. Locking the main door he crossed the hall to the lifts. Up on the fourth floor landing he saw himself reflected in the dark window. He was all cuts and bruises, stitches to the head, torn shirt. He grinned.

Should have seen the other fucker.

He went into his flat, not bothering with the lights. He switched the television on and poured himself a drink, then levered himself out of his chair. He relaxed on the settee. He'd been in a fight, a real one. That stuff in the theatre earlier seemed miles away now. He'd really fucked a couple of those bastards up. He laughed and picked up the phone, dialling a number. As the number rang out he thought hard, then made up his mind.

"Hi, are you still taking orders? OK, I'd like a large

Marguerita with extra anchovies and a bottle of Pepsi," he said.

"Andrew, stop pissing about and just tell me," Julie said.

Andrew looked hurt. "I will now," he said, sternly. "Hang on." He rolled the dice again, got a one and a six. "Nearly there that time," he grinned, scratching his forehead.

"Sorry mate, how does this work again?" Philip asked.

"If I roll an eight in eight rolls or less," Andrew said, "I tell you about Mick."

He was shaking the dice in his cupped hand, blowing on them as they clicked against his signet ring. A tiny bluebird was tattooed on his hand, with CCFC on a banner flapping around his thumb.

"But what's the fucking point?" Julie said.

Andrew looked hurt again. "This is how I do all my business. Now shut up."

Julie rolled her eyes at Philip, who grinned.

"What do you want Mick for anyway?" Julie asked.

"Well, you know," Philip said. "Business."

Andrew nodded approvingly and rolled. The dice bounced off the ashtray, and came up with two fours.

"Sorted!" Andrew said.

"Spot on," said Philip. "So Mick..."

"Well, Mick's this weird little fucker, dresses weird, you know, like a punk or whatever."

Andrew looked at Philip. "Like you. He's got something fucked with him, he says his mother smoked too much when she was having him. That's why he looks like he does. But he goes out a lot with the boys, comes up here with them and that. He don't really get on with them, he's a weird little fucker."

"Why does he hang around with them then?"

Andrew looked around, then came closer. "Mick likes his drugs see. Gets them off Minty and all that lot."

He nodded and sat back, playing with his dice.

Philip smiled. "So he's here tonight, then?"

"Yeah, he's over there."

He left Julie dancing and went and stood in the passage.

Two boys were playing on the bandit while a couple dry-humped each other over the cloakroom counter. A bald man in a Pringle sweater and a huge gold chain wandered in, looking for his fare. Philip lit a fag and watched Helen scurry from the toilets and out to the taxi in her bare feet, clutching her stilettoes.

This bloke, Mick, was over with some heavy looking bastards. If he was into drugs they'd be Minty's mob. Bollocks. That was the only fucking growth industry in the bloody valleys. And Minty was the bloody M.D. All their girls, however many he'd taken by now, all swore not to tell. It would be just as bad for them. And there he was, bringing a bit of fey into the bedrooms of the macho, the valley's amphetamine aristocracy. Which was fine as far as ridiculous, obsessive missions went, but this was about as far as it did go.

So now it was time to talk to Emma. But he had to talk to Mick first, who was obviously sorting his drugs out with people whose girlfriends Philip had probably drifted into and out of again. He decided to wait until Mick went to the bog.

Fuck the shotgun, the words that meant fuck all; bollocks to the theatre, bollocks to all theatres, to those English ponces, to all the English, bollocks to creative writing and bollocks to hair gel. He'd get Philip and they'd go around Cardiff pubs together. Yeah, and if there was any shit, he'd lay into the bastards. Like tonight, fucking right. That was the real thing.

Jason, on the settee, started drooping until his head was in the pizza box. The cardboard corner hurt his ear so he shoved it out of the way. Somewhere on the way to sleep he'd pulled his trainers off, and now he stretched out on the settee and started snoring.

A bloke came out of the bogs, cracking his knuckles and chuckling. Then another followed, holding a wad of toilet paper to his bloody nose.

"I never said she was fat," he mumbled.

Philip hurried into the toilets and stood behind the condom machine. He'd seen Mick get up and start across the dancefloor. He read the condom machine while he waited.

Mick came in. He looked different up close. Like someone had filed his shoulders down to rounded hubs. His chest curved inwards, and his head was too big. Philip watched him take a piss. Christ, he had a massive prick, though. Jason was right, God's a bastard.

When he finished, Mick turned and saw Philip.

"Hello," Philip said.

"How much do you want?" Mick said, his eyes wide.

"No, you're OK."

"What's the problem then?"

"No problem, really. Can we have a chat?"

"In here?"

"In the passage?"

"OK."

They stood near the exit, trying not to look at the frottage couple.

"You're a friend of Emma's," Philip said.

"Emma? Yeah, she's my friend."

"I met her once," Philip said. "I liked her. A lot. I'd like to see her again."

"Nice one. She likes visitors." Mick turned to go.

"Mick, look, I mean, is she...?"

"Is she what? What have you heard?" Mick was all ears suddenly, a nasty look on his face.

"Nothing, I haven't heard anything. I just mean, you know, what does she do?"

"Nothing. She's on the dole."

"Why doesn't she ever come out?"

"I suppose she doesn't want to."

"Well, look, why do all people go to her house?"

Mick looked really pissed off now. "To fuck each other and take drugs when they think she's not looking. To pretend to be her friends."

"Why does she put up with it? She didn't seem to like them much, that one time I was there."

"She gets lonely. Look, who the fuck are you, anyway, like?"

"Look, she's into Bowie, yeah? Well, I've got this tape of

132

rarities, really hard-to-get stuff, I thought she might like a listen, you know. But I don't want to turn up there, like last time."

Mick scratched his neck, and Philip could just see he had a scar running down his throat and under his shirt. A proper, surgical scar.

"She likes Bowie, yeah," Mick said. "I'll be going back there later, with some of the boys. They won't hang around for long though. You can come in the car with us."

"Uh, yeah...I can't really do that, see."

"Why not?"

"I don't really get on with them, you know."

"Well, whatever."

"Look, how about if I just walk back there, and you could mention I might come over?"

"Walk? All the way from here?"

"Well, I'll get a taxi or whatever."

"Mate, if you want to crash round Emma's, just do it. You won't be the first, like."

"No but... OK, yeah, I'll just turn up then."

"Whatever. Catch you later."

He went back in. Philip hovered in the passage. It was getting on for eleven. If he started walking now, he could be there by about midnight. Mick should be there then, and the others might have left. He'd been stupid. The valley was small enough already, without him making it smaller for himself by pissing everybody off. He looked through to the dancefloor and saw Julie dancing with her friends. He shrugged. She would have been the last anyway. He walked out of Seventh Heaven into the drizzle.

In her vanilla scented bedroom, Claire fiddled with her pyjama buttons. She was asleep and dreaming of Jason. He kept getting out of his wheelchair to nose around her room. She was trying to tell him something important but he just kept getting up and poking around, picking things off her shelves, flicking through her CDs, reading her notes.

She got really annoyed with him and he just laughed at her,

then reared up and pushed her down on to her bed. His stubble was rubbing up against her neck, hurting her. She was struggling, his weight pressing down, struggling to get her blouse open, to let him get what he wanted. Outside, through her window, she could see an airliner, far too low, silently cruising past. Some of the passengers glanced in at her.

Gone midnight. He was trudging along, half-asleep, up through the valley. The drizzle was heavy, you couldn't make anything out. Just smeared orange lights dripping down the sky, weak and pissy. He tried to keep his eyes up, looking ahead of him, but the rain and his tiredness made them drop down, to focus on his boots and they plodded on.

Then, looking up, he saw he was on the estate at last. He didn't usually have occasion to come up here. Bit stupid really. He bit his lip. Plenty of people up here would take time out to kick his head in. He stumbled over the brow of the hill and looked down over the estate. That was the house, he was pretty sure, where this fucking sex odyssey had started. Perhaps he'd made the wrong choice that night, going for the Debbies and Helens instead of Emma. Whatever. He couldn't even remember why he was here now. What he'd thought he'd find here.

Her house took on sharp edges out of the gloom, but it wasn't until he was at the gate that he saw Emma. She was leaning on her windowsill, blowing cigarette smoke out into the night.

This was a fantasy. There was nothing but the long trudge home. There was no girl waiting there for him.

Emma tilted her head as she looked over at him, then nodded at the front door and disappeared. Philip stood by the gate, looking around. Her front door opened and she stood there, waiting for him. He opened the gate and walked through the small garden, then followed her into the house.

10. SEPTEMBER 1993.

After Val dropped Joan off at work, he felt it again – that thing that opened up, like a big pit, under his slippers. The sight of them, resting on the damp rubber mat under the car's pedals, made him wince. Cheery tartan. When he looked up, through the windscreen, and saw the street stretching out ahead, it hit him. Time, that's what he thought it was. Half eight on a weekday morning and he was looking down the main road, past the station, past the theatre, the big billboards by the police houses, the cafe and chip shop, down to the traffic lights at Stag Square. And all that would still be there at nine, at ten, at eleven, all afternoon, into the night, and Val could still be sitting here looking at it.

He drove back to the house. No wonder Philip stayed in bed until the afternoon. This must be how the world looked to him. Just like Jason had said. Streets stretching ahead of you, for hours on end, with no particular reason for you to go down them. They went from being corridors, taking you to work and other important places, to being streets, silly, long streets, full of things happening for no reason, people and cars, weather and time. They didn't stop you travelling along them, these streets, but suddenly they didn't complain or even notice if you didn't. The town turned into just streets, so did the whole valley.

At the house, Claire was getting ready for school. She had her tie on and was sorting out her bag, so small and neat.

"All right, love?" Val said.

She nodded and smiled.

"Don't forget this," he said, handing her a letter he'd picked up from the table. It was addressed to Jason, in Claire's writing.

"Thanks," she said, taking it from him.

Val watched her put the letter in her bag. He couldn't think of a way to tell her how important she was, and not to get bogged down, so he said nothing and let her get off. Then he sat down and switched the television on, trying to find some news.

"What shall we do now?" Philip said.

"David Morgan's?" Jason said.

"The blood capsules?"

"Why not?"

They headed off down The Hayes to the department store, past the winos in their grey suits and white Hi-Tec trainers.

"That's how I'll end up," Jason said, "picking fights, shouting obscenities, drinking Brasso and pissing my pants."

"So, no change there then," Philip smirked.

"You really are a wanker, Phil, you know? I meant everything I said. You're OK as long as you're not talking. Or writing. Or using words in any way at all. You're quite cute as long as you keep your mouth shut, but as soon as words come out of you it becomes horribly clear what a little wanker you really are."

"Shut up and concentrate," Philip said. "Here come the revolving doors."

They cut a swathe through the ground floor shoppers in David Morgan, pushing past them as they browsed through tiny crystal swans and cut-glass pot pourri containers.

Through the cravats and dress jewellery they went, and into the lift.

"Stand clear, doors closing," the lift said.

A middle aged couple were in there with them, on their way to eat pastries in the Top of the Shop restaurant.

"Claire's been trying to ring you," Philip said.

Jason said nothing.

"The drama thing's on hold. I'm not writing it. I've been a bit busy."

"Yeah, shagging," Jason grunted.

The middle aged couple looked at each other.

"No, I've packed that in now. I've been trying to sort my Dad out some jobs, you know, playing in pubs. And there's Emma and Mick."

"Your new friends."

"You've got to meet them."

"Whatever."

"Stand clear, doors opening," the lift said.

They made their way past the mirrors, lamps and oil paintings to the Top of the Shop.

They got two glasses of iced water from the machine and sat down in the smoking section. An electric piano and orchestra version of *Eleanor Rigby* drifted through the restaurant, snagging on the chandeliers. Philip watched a woman with lacquered hair tapping her red nails on her capuccino cup. On the next table a gang of bright young things with interesting sunglasses ironically enjoyed the ambience as they chatted in their faux-English accents about doing some work for BBC Wales. The couple from the lift came and sat opposite, picking at their pastries as they talked about house prices in Rhiwbina.

"So what's she been saying then?" Jason said.

"Hmm?"

"Claire."

"She wants to know what you've been doing."

"Been down the group a bit."

"Yeah? What's it like?"

"Well, their main aim seems to be wheelchair adornment."

"What?"

"Wheelchair adornment. They encourage you to put stickers all over your chair."

"What sort of stickers?"

Jason shrugged.

"'Radio 1 Roadshow'. 'Hot Willie's Surf Shack, Penzance'. 'Smile if you had sex last night'. 'My other car's a...'"

"Oh, fuck off," Philip gasped.

"No, straight up," Jason said. "Stickers."

Philip shook his head and whistled.

"Listen," Jason said, "one bloke there, Simon, he's got these things on his spokes, y'know, them multi-coloured plastic things that go clack when you move. You know, like girls have on their bikes."

"Jesus."

"Then you get the sporty ones," Jason went on, waving his

arms around. "They take the arms off their chairs so they can reach the wheels better, and wear those gloves, like Tour de France cyclists."

"Lots of sportswear?"

"Jogging bottoms, Reeboks. Some lycra."

"Neat."

"And they're always having discussions about what to call themselves. They're not handicapped, not disabled, not physically challenged, not differently abled..."

"And certainly not crippled?"

"No, they're not over-keen on that."

"Claire wanted to know if you got her letter." Philip said.

Jason lit a fag and said, "Yeah, I got it."

"She wants to see you."

"I know."

Jason looked up at the chandelier above them, then out of the window, past the curlicues of the building, and saw a little man on the street, opposite Argos, bending down to pick something up, and stumbling to his knees. Jason grinned as the little man hurriedly got to his feet and adjusted his clothing, brushing down his hair as he looked guiltily around him and scurried off. Jason turned back to Philip, smiling.

"You can tell her she'll see me soon," he said. "Very soon. I'm coming back up to Treorchy, to see her."

Philip raised his eyebrows.

"I've got to, haven't I?" Jason said "Got to do the stupid dance again. Because I want to be suave."

"You want to be what?" Philip said.

"Suave. I don't want to be scruffy. Like you. I like looking good, shaving, having neat hair, wearing nice clothes, being suave. So I'll have to go back, won't I?" He grinned and winked.

"I don't understand you," Philip said. "You're like some kind of monkey or something."

"Fuck that noise," Jason said, "just get the blood capsules out."

Philip put the paper bag on the table and took out the fake blood capsules from the joke shop in the arcade.

"Right, here we go," Jason said, putting them in his mouth and biting. Fake blood started dribbling down his chin.

"Aaaargh, shit, aaargh, oh God!" he cried.

"Shit, shit, help," Philip said. "Someone please help him!"

Philip grabbed the chair and they careered around the Top of the Shop, shouting and screaming.

"Aaaargh!" Jason shouted, spraying blood over the next table, where the bright young things paused in waving their long cigarettes around and froze.

"Don't touch the salad, for God's sake!" Philip shouted at the couple with the pastries.

A waitress dropped her plate.

After a lap of the restaurant they escaped in the lift and were strolling down the street in the cool air.

"What now?" Philip asked.

Jason wiped his mouth and said, "Let's go for a pint. This stuff tastes fucking horrible."

Jason decided to go back to Treorchy with Philip that night, just to see what happened. They were quiet on the train up from Cardiff, with the commuters snoring all around them. The two of them gazed through the windows. Suave, Jason thought. He'd actually used that word. And it did mean something to him, however strange it sounded. He watched the suburban allotments flash by, the trees and bridges, and felt something starting in his head, flashing too, really barrelling along, coming into view.

He thought about Claire first, with her glowing skin and shiny hair, the little angel, sent by God to make sure he joined in the dance, jerking his strings. It was that or hide in the flat – lie down on the mattress, get fat, and die slowly, watching videos. You either danced or died, that was the deal. OK, so that was Claire.

The train bounced as it hurtled over the points at Taff's Well, then accelerated away, the lamp-posts going flash-past, flash-past, flash-past, and Jason thought. What picked away at him was this thing Phil had started talking about – the third way.

Phil meant that the bad guys were one, the good guys were two. So, in real life, Minty and his mob were one, the snoring commuters were two. They each knew what they were, and either went to dodgy clubs or karaoke evenings, and that was that. They both look down their nose at me, at us, Phil had said. So he wanted a third way of being, because he was neither one nor two, he wanted to be something different in the valley. The way he talked, since this business with Emma, meant he must have found it, or thought he had.

But, but, but – Jason had to stay on track here, follow the words as they rushed into the light – but for Jason the third way meant something else. If dancing the spastic dance was one, then blanking out and waiting for it to end was two. But sometimes, yes, thinking back to his times with Claire, he could almost envisage a third way.

When, then? Specifically? And what were the elements? It was when he felt in control and then he was, well, suave. Stupid word but fuck it – it would do. It was like his old fantasy, walking into the bar, being one cool bastard. Sometimes that did happen in 'real life, even with the wheelchair and everything, he felt just like that. When he thought back to those times, thought really hard, like now, like never before in fact, he knew that the wheelchair was part of it. Yes, that being Jason the cripple was part and parcel of feeling like he did on those occasions, cool and sexy and hard and suave. A fucking shocking thought, to Jason the un-shockable.

But yes, it was there, it was true. He stared out of the window, not seeing the world flashing by now, but feeling it, rushing at him and past. He had to concentrate as the images went by, see what details they were made up of, how it all fitted in, what picture it made.

So all he had to do was figure out a formula for the feeling, the suave feeling. And then? Then the third way would rise up out of nowhere, and he'd have the fucker beaten.

Part of it was the sex thing, that was obvious. Because whatever plans Claire had, whatever bunch of shit she cooked up with her community arts pals, deep down she just wanted him. Like in his flat, begging him to do it to her. It wasn't nice, fuck, it was horrible – to be proud of that. But it was just proof, that it was more than just sympathy and compassion and all that do-gooder shit. Claire was into him – fact. Sex appeal was the first element then.

Swearing had to be the second. He grinned. Pissing people off. Like at Martin's group, or in pubs, or with the blood capsules earlier. Maybe that wasn't anything to be proud of either. But it made him feel good – why? Another shocking thought: that crap Phil wrote for him, for the play – it wasn't that far off. He did see it like that – victim of the cosmic joke, the underdog, with a mission to show up the whole sham for what it was – a deliberately ugly and stupid dance, to show up the big dance. Fuck, there were plenty of precedents for this type of thing.

And when he was on a roll, really going for it, he felt shit-hot, he had that twisted charisma, Christ, he knew it, he was suave. He was biting his nails now, excited and nervous.

But it had to be real, that was what was wrong with the play, that fake anger bullshit. It had to be him and it had to be real. This was leading somewhere, it had to be.

Finish the formula, don't start admiring it until it's done. The suave feeling, then, came from being like that, telling it like it was, that attitude; and that fed back into the sex appeal. And then, the biggest, shockingest, most dizzying thought of all: the attitude led to the suave, which led to the sex appeal, completely by-passing the legs, and – potentially – even going beyond Claire herself. He stared wildly around the carriage at the slack faces, side partings, paperback novels. Beyond Claire...

Fuck, fuck, fuck, he thought, and a parallel track went no, hold on, hold on, hold on. If – he thought, slowly and carefully, forcing himself to spell the words out – if this formula worked in real life...but he lost it, and his mind raced on, jabbering away about whether this was really important or not, or what; and did it mean anything, really, and could you beat the bastards, really, like this, was this the solution, could it work; and how stupid was all this excitement anyway, was it just gearing him up to get back on the dancefloor and try, try, try again, and fail spectacularly as he was bound to, and look the stupidest, ugliest, crappest, most pathetic, crippled bastard on Earth, and remind him that it was he himself who'd done this, flushed his pride down the bog for the oldest trick in the book, after swearing never again.

He slumped back in the chair, exhausted. He looked over at Phil, who was staring ahead of him. He had a very slight smile on his lips, lost in his own thoughts. Jason couldn't think of the details anymore: it was all wrapped up in a tight little elastic band ball, bouncing around his bruised skull – but not unravelling.

They got off the train at Treorchy, Philip bumping the wheelchair down on to the platform. He noticed that the station's litter bin, which used to hang on the railings, was now a crusty yellow pancake on the floor. No trace of its former shape or function remained. Plastic was so adaptable.

As they passed Mr Snooker's a boy dodged past them and disappeared inside.

"See him, then?" Philip said.

"Yeah."

"Name's Corky. He's afraid of blood. Won't touch his girl-friend when she's on. I had her a few months ago, in the bogs at The Blacksmith."

"You filthy little bastard," Jason said, "I don't want to know the details."

Someone came up to them, sneaking up from behind, Jason thought.

"Watch out," he hissed.

Philip spun around, then smiled, seeing it was Emma's friend.

"Hiya Mick, how's it going?" he said.

"Fucking awful, I just had a re-start interview," Mick said. "Last time I put my job preferences down I knew I'd be in the shit: I just put Evel Kneivel, Judge Dredd and Shaun Ryder. Said I'd be happy doing any of them jobs. It was OK because they had that drippy bloke doing it, and he tried to translate them into real jobs, so it was like: dispatch rider, police force or musician. This time the guy just threatened to cut off my dole, so I had to make up new ones there and then. And all I could think of was court usher."

"Court usher?" Philip said.

"Well, yeah, because I know the drill off by heart after being up so many times. Well, the tosser's only gone and arranged a week's ET down the court, ain't he?"

Mick grinned suddenly. "So I'm determined to smoke a joint in the magistrate's bogs. That's for definite."

"Well, you've got to have goals," Philip said.

Mick nodded and looked at Jason.

"All right, mate?" Jason said.

"Do I look all right?" Mick sneered.

Jason practically did a double-take, Philip noticed. The truth was, Mick looked far from all right. He looked like his mother had been taking funny pills when she was having him. But Jason was obviously a bit put-out, and that was funny.

"What's in the bag?" Jason grunted, trying to gain some ground.

Mick just reached casually into the bag and took out his training weights.

"Twelve pounds each," he said, handing one to Jason, who hefted it above his head, staring all the time at Mick.

"Trying to straighten yourself out?" Jason said.

Philip gasped and shot a glance at Mick.

"Bit late for that," Mick shrugged, hefting the other weight. "It's just so when I hit some fucker who gives me shit, I know he's going to go down."

"Fists of steel, is it?" Jason smirked.

"No," Mick said. "I hit them with one of these."

Then they both burst out laughing, so Philip joined in too.

They went to The Railway for a drink, and squeezed into a corner table. It was still early, but Philip knew all about The Railway, its sudden surges of business at odd hours, how people only pretended to pop in for a quick pint. Sometimes they just came in, did a lap of the bar, then went back out.

Minty's new BMW was usually parked around the corner, and the pub was often referred to obliquely in the *Rhondda Leader*. It was only a matter of time before it got closed, then it would be some other place further up the valley.

"You know about Einstein here and his clever hobby?" Mick said.

Jason nodded. "He tells me all the details."

"Who's next on the hit list, McKay?"

Phil shrugged, drank his lager. Mick leaned towards Jason.

"The way I reckon it," he said, "there's only one left now, on the big score sheet, like."

"What, Minty's bird?" Jason said.

"For Christ's sake, Jase," Philip hissed. "Not so loud, not in here."

"Stupid hobby anyway," Jason said.

"I've packed it in now, haven't I?" Philip said.

"Fair play," Mick said, "it's a bloody stupid way to spend your nights, like, agreed. But to pack it in now, before the cup final?" He shook his lumpy head.

"Yeah." Jason grinned, putting his arm on Philip's shoulders. "You'll only ever be number two seed."

Mick spluttered into his pint. Philip had a nervous look around the room, but it seemed OK. He felt quite good, right at this moment. The three of them had colonised this corner of the pub: there was the bag of stuff he'd taken down Jason's, there was Mick's carrier bag, and there was Jason's wheelchair, all marking this corner off as theirs. And there were the three of them, cackling over secrets in The Railway. He could see them in the mirror on the far wall, and a right freak show they looked, just like Minty said. This could be good.

Kelvin Nussbaum was driving to the all-night garage to get some Golden Virginia. He was staying with Dee-Dee, who had just bought a house in Ystrad. She said life in the valley was so much more relaxed than in London. Kelvin agreed, but said he couldn't imagine not living within walking distance of an alternative cabaret venue.

It was gone eleven and he was singing along to The

Levellers as Glyndwr tried to lick melted Kit-Kat from his fingers. Dee-Dee wouldn't have the dog in the house without Kelvin, as it tended to panic and make a mess.

"Glyndwr, leave it out!"

Kelvin snatched his hand from the gear stick and put it back on the wheel. When he looked up again he thought he'd accidentally driven into a street carnival. There were youngsters everywhere, girls in short skirts holding beer bottles and dancing in front of his headlights, groups of boys earnestly discussing things right in the middle of the road. He dropped his speed to five miles an hour and picked his way past minibuses and taxis and kids drumming on his roof. Glyndwr whined.

He pulled into the garage forecourt and walked through the crowds to the kiosk. It was like crossing a dance floor. A couple were sitting by the petrol pumps, having an argument. He joined the queue. Behind the bullet-proof glass a man in his sixties was trying to deal with the punters. He was obviously a bit deaf, and they were slurring as they shouted through the glass. Kelvin listened to them.

"Twenty Bensons, you deaf old fucker."

"I'm sorry, young man?"

"Fucking hell..."

"No, two cheese and onion, one salt and vinegar and a ham and chives, I said."

"What have I got here?"

"Two salt and vinegar, one cheese and onion and a chargrilled beef."

"I'm so sorry, I'll just go and change them."

"No, it don't matter, give 'em here...fuck, too late."

"Twenty Lambert and Butler and a packet of Rizlas."

"Pack of Royals and a pint of milk. And some green Rizlas."

"Some crisps and some skins."

"Here we are then, two ham and chives, two salt and vinegar and a cheese and onion."

"Jesus Christ..."

"Twenty Bensons."

"Twenty ...?"

"BENSONS! Fucksake…"

"You two, have you been served? Can you move away then please. Now then, young man?"

A man behind Kelvin was getting very annoyed.

"For fuck's sake, we'll be here till fucking Christmas. I'll be as fucking old as him. Boys! Where you off? Hang on a minute, I'm getting fags! Hang on, you fucking waster bastards!"

He pushed in front of Kelvin, who was next, and shouldered him out of the queue.

"Twenty Lamberts."

"I'm sorry?"

"Lamberts! Fucking hell."

The man turned to look at Kelvin.

"You got a fucking problem mate?" he said.

"No, no," Kelvin shrugged, stepping back.

"Well fucking stop pushing then."

Kelvin had been in tricky situations before, on picket lines and demos. Some had got pretty nasty. But there was always a sense of us-against-them. It made something like a black eye OK. This was different though, so blank, so meaningless. You could get stabbed here for just standing in a queue. He shook his head. How far down did you have to dig to find the community here? It was worse than he thought, the place had been totally brutalised.

"Yes, young man?"

"A packet of Golden Virginia and some Rizlas, please," Kelvin said.

He walked back to the car, past a boy in a day-glo orange T-shirt pissing in a water bucket. Just as he opened his door a short kid came bobbing up to him.

"All right, butty?" he said.

He was very small and had a crew cut. Kelvin smiled at him.

"Where you off then?" the kid said.

"I'm just going home," Kelvin stuttered.

"Are you going down that way? Any chance of a lift? Please, like?" the kid said.

He was bobbing around and looked very humble.

"I've, er, I've got a passenger," Kelvin said, pointing at the dog in the two-door's passenger seat.

"S'all right," the kid smiled, "I do love dogs, I do."

"Look, I'm not going very far..."

The kid looked at the tobacco and rolling papers in Kelvin's hand. Then he lowered his voice.

"Can you spare us a blim?" he said.

Kelvin looked lost.

"A little bit of blow. Just a blim. C'mon, like, is it?"

"No, this is just for tobacco," Kelvin said.

"Just a blim, like. Just enough for a spliff. Half a spliff. Is it?"

Kelvin ran a hand through his hair, looked around, frowned. He genuinely didn't know what to do, how to end this. Then there was a shout and the boy looked around.

"Oi, Titch!"

It was Mick, coming along the forecourt with Philip and Jason.

"You begging again, you little urchin?" Mick said.

"Kelvin, you old bastard!" Philip shouted.

Glyndwr started whining again.

"Any chance of a blim, Mick? Just a spliff?" Titch said.

"Away from the cameras," Mick said, rifling through his bag, and they went around the corner.

"How's it going, Kelvin?" Philip said.

"Fine, yeah, great. Haven't seen much of you two lately. How are you, Jason?"

"Spiffing, mate, fucking spiffing." Jason was drinking from a beer bottle and looking very cocky.

"I was talking to Claire earlier," Kelvin said. "The play seems to be dying on its feet, sadly. People just won't get involved."

"Apart from pissing through the letter box," Jason said.

"Well, that's it, isn't it? I wish they'd just come in, y'know, see what it's all about."

Philip and Jason looked at each other.

"What about you two?" Kelvin said. "Fancy giving it another try?"

They looked at each other again, exchanging raised eyebrows and grins.

"We may take an interest," Philip said.

"Yeah, we might have something fresh to contribute."

"Might be quite soon."

"Could well be."

"But there'd have to be a few changes," Jason said. "I think we need to re-orientate the focus of the project as a whole."

Philip sniggered into his beer bottle.

"Well, y'know, Claire is very open to..."

"We'll see," Jason nodded.

Philip giggled and Mick came back over.

"Come on then boys," he said, "let's get going. It's a bit cold for this kind of activity."

"See you, Kelvin," Philip said as they moved off.

"Yes, make it soon."

"Could happen," Jason said.

Kelvin shook his head, and went to get into the car. A crew cut appeared in front of him.

"So, about that lift, then?" Titch said.

Jason shifted in his chair, and drops of rain from the leaves ran down his arms.

"How much longer?" he asked.

"Shouldn't be long now," Phil said.

They were hiding in the bushes at the side of Emma's house, waiting for Mick to give the all clear. When they got there a car was parked outside, and Phil got scared. Mick went in to suss things out, and now Jason was freezing.

Phil put his hand on the wheelchair to lever himself into a better position, then settled again, gazing at the house. His black hair glistened with tiny rain bubbles as he squatted there, watching. He was facing away from Jason, who found himself looking at the round pebble of bone at the top of his friend's neck, between his collar and where his hair started. His black jacket was starting to fade, with white lines rippling across it. Jason had a swig from his hipflask and nudged Phil's shoulder, offering it to him. Phil took it and drank, then handed it back. They didn't even acknowledge each other when they passed the hipflask, Jason noticed, not even a smile of thanks. They

148

didn't need to. They had become like brothers, Jason thought, and he felt very fond of old Phil then.

Some boys came out of Emma's house, got into the car and drove off.

"Hey, Phil," Jason said.

He turned to look at Jason.

"When are you going to grow up and get a job?"

"Never," Phil said, with a little sneer.

Jason laughed and ruffled his friend's hair. Phil gave him a strange look, then Mick appeared.

"All clear," he said, and they trooped into the house.

"I sold Mick some blow the other day," Corky said as he drove the car away from Emma's house and back down the hill.

"You got to watch him," Lufty said. "I saw him earlier on, dealing."

"What, Mick?"

"Yeah, fucking right. By the Action garage. Selling some blow to this little kid."

"Serious? Fucking cunt. I sold him eight quid's worth, right, and he probably sold it on for about a tenner. Them little kids don't know no fucking different."

"Aye, but Mick's only made two quid, haven't he?"

"Yeah, but if he does that every fucking time, like," Corky said. "It all adds up, don't it? That's two quid less for me, like, every time."

"That's how they fucking start."

"Fucking twat reckons he's going into business, like."

They both laughed.

"He goes around with that weird fucker, don't he?" Lufty said.

"Who's that?"

"Skinny fucker, goes around with that spastic."

"Oh, that fucker. Always sniffing around, like. He's looking for a slapping too."

"Next time we see them."

"Fucking right."

Emma had short, dark hair and stood staring at the wall when they came in. She took a drag on her cigarette then turned suddenly to face them.

"The bastards took two of my fucking pictures," she said pointing.

Jason looked at the wall above her fireplace. It was covered with postcards, photocopies, pictures torn from books, photographs. There had to be three hundred of them. Each was about three inches from the other. Emma was obviously working from the right to the left. The two gaps above the mantelpiece were glaring.

"You shouldn't let the fuckers in here," Mick said, slamming the living room door behind Jason.

"What else am I supposed to do, Mick?" Emma said.

"I don't know," Mick said. "Any fucking thing."

Jason couldn't understand what the fuss was about, and he turned to Phil, who just shrugged. So Jason looked at the wall, at the Eschers and the Dalis, the Robert Crumb cartoons and 2000 AD characters, at posters warning against careless talk, incendiary bombs and Jews, at a woman floating on her back down a dark river, holding flowers, and another woman in a white gown sitting in a boat, floating down what looked like the same river. There were black and white photos of brides and grooms and babies, pictures of outer space, people arguing and pointing while a bearded God in red perched on a cloud just above their heads. He saw a glowing green forest with what looked like linguini growing out of the ground, and a mermaid holding an oversized hot water bottle. He counted at least thirteen crucifixions and a lot of paintings by the man who designed *Alien*. And, just above the mantelpiece, two rectangles of faded yellow with streaks of white. He moved closer, touched the gaps where the two missing pictures had been. His fingers traced the white streaks on the wall.

"This is paper," he said, then ran his hand across the pictures. "These are glued." He looked at the others with a frown. "These are all glued to the wall."

"Exactly," Emma said. "They ripped them right off."

Jason was about to ask why she didn't use Blu-tac when Phil

150

nudged him and shook his head. This was fucking nuts. He knew Phil liked the company of freaks, but Emma was just a psycho. Phil and Mick were treating her like she was a princess, but as far as he could see she was just a nutter.

Mick slouched into an armchair and Phil sat next to the coal fire and started going through his bag for some David Bowie tapes. Emma cheered up a bit then and got them some drinks. She didn't turn the light on and they sat in the orange glow of the fire, and it felt like they were camping, huddled together in the deepest part of the forest, away from everyone.

By two, Phil and Mick were vodka'd out, flat on their backs and snoring.

"That's them gone then," Jason said, feeling drunkenly cosy.

"Well, they're only little," Emma said, smiling at them. "I don't know about you, but I'm having another one."

Jason held his glass out. "Do you know where we met, me and Phil?" he said, feeling all affectionate again.

"On holiday," Emma said. "He pushed you away from a castle."

Jason laughed. "Yeah. Bet he wishes he hadn't now."

"Why?"

"Ah, well, fuck it, y'know." Jason drank some vodka and looked up to see Emma still looking at him. "Well, he could be all set up by now. Nice job, steady girlfriend."

Emma looked puzzled.

"What?" Jason said. "You mean what's it got to do with me?"

She shrugged.

"It is to do with me though. I thought he'd just hang around for a while until he got sick of it, then go to college or whatever. But he's still buggering about." He looked up at Emma, gave a little smile. "This probably don't make any sense to you."

"I know he wants to be like you."

"Oh fuck..." Jason grinned.

"He's OK, though, Philip."

"Oh yeah, he's OK."

They talked for a while about other stuff, and she showed him all her Carry On films, dozens of them stacked up in the cabinet on the wall, then her Nick Cave albums, and he laughed at the contrast in her tastes.

"I'll play you two of my favourite songs," she said, and scurried over to the stereo.

Quietly, so they wouldn't wake the others, they listened to a Birthday Party song which began, "I stuck a six inch gold blade into the neck of a girl." Jason made funny grimaces at her, and she wrinkled her nose and laughed. Then she put on a song by The Shadows, called *Foot Tapper*, smiling and shaking her head to the simple jauntiness bouncing direct from 1962 into her flat.

"I've always been funny in the head," she said, taking the tape out of the deck. She turned to him, smiling. "When I was thirteen I broke a copper's nose."

"Yeah?"

She nodded. "But the funny thing is why I did it."

"Why?"

"He tried to take a pigs tea-towel off me."

"What?"

"He tried to take a pigs tea-towel off me."

"What the fuck's a pigs tea-towel?"

"It's what he thought I was stealing from Woolworths. A tea-towel with pigs on it."

"Drawings of pigs?"

"Well, yeah, not real ones. Cartoon pigs."

"And were you stealing it?"

"No, I'd already paid, but I was tucking it in my jacket as I was walking out of the shop."

"Tucking it in your jacket?"

"I never carried a bag. Still don't."

"So what happened?"

"He came on to me as I was going to cross the road, and grabbed my elbow, so I hit him."

Jason grinned. This was the kind of tale he could relate to. "Yeah?" he said.

"Broke his nose."

"Strange," Jason said.

"I was surprised."

"What pissed you off so much, then?"

"I don't know really. I'd had a bad day, Christmas shopping. My father had given me some money, and my gran had given me money, so I went to Ponty to buy presents. My gran likes things with pigs on them, see, she's got loads of stuff. And I saw this tea-towel, with all these pigs on it."

"What were they doing?"

"Who?"

"The pigs."

"I don't know. Just talking."

Jason threw back his head and laughed.

"Ssh, you'll wake them up. Anyway, everything was going wrong that day, I missed the train, and this fat sod stepped on my foot, you know how narrow the pavements are in Ponty? And the rain was pissing on me, and I couldn't find anything for my father..." she sighed.

"I hate days like that," Jason said.

"The thing is, I hate all that, but I really hate buying crap presents. It's got to be something they want. I feel shitty otherwise. Well, when the copper came on to me I just thought, fuck it, I'm doing my best, aren't I? What more can I do, like? And that was it."

"What happened?"

"I went to court. My mother got fined. My grandmother got the tea-towel. I got an electronic keyboard. I started drinking. I stopped going to school. I went with a lot of boys. I ended up here."

Jason tried to see if she was joking. "All because you hit a copper?"

She shook her head, not smiling, looking tired. "What's the point trying to work out why about everything? You'll never know, and it won't make any difference anyway."

She shrugged. "Fuck it."

She lit a cigarette and turned to gaze at the pictures on her wall as they flickered in the firelight.

"Emma," Jason said, "why don't you use Blu-tac?"

He could tell, it must have been some tiny movement in her shoulders, that she'd heard, and that the question was bigger than he thought. He shifted in his chair and she turned back towards him.

"Why should I?" she said.

"Well, then if you move you can take them with you."

"But I'm not moving," she said. "I'll never move out of this flat."

She was staring at him – not at him though, just towards him. Her face was as blank as copper. He didn't know what to say, and he could taste vodka in his throat.

"How can you be sure you won't move?" he said at last.

"Some things you can be sure of," she said. She reached out and touched his leg, squeezed it just above the knee. "You won't never walk. Never ever ever." She shook her head slowly. "I won't never move out of here. Never ever."

"It's like that, is it?" Jason said.

"Yeah, just like that. It's in black and white. So that's the end of that one. What do you want to talk about now?"

Emma pulled the quilt over and drew her legs up under her. She looked over at the three boys sleeping, Mick on the other armchair, Philip on the floor by the fire, Jason flat out on the settee. Three bad, bad little boys, she thought, fast asleep now. Where else would they be, if not here, and what would they be doing? She slid her watch off and put it on the floor.

Nearly four now, and she still couldn't sleep. The vodka was gone, and all she felt was dizzy. She curled up in the chair and looked at her pictures. The council would have a hard job stripping all them off. And they'd have to. Paint or wallpaper would get lumpy. They would have to scrub away at each one individually. The workmen would be there for a long time, looking at each picture she had stuck there as they scrubbed and scraped them away. She looked at each picture in turn, imagining how they would look, what the workmen would think of the girl who had lived here. Then, letting her mind drift, she looked at the women, Ophelia and the one in the boat, floating off down the river, their hair trailing behind them, through the weeds and petals, off into the dark; and after a long time, Emma went with them, finally asleep.

11. OCTOBER 1993.

ANOTHER OF LIFE'S CRAPPY IRONIES

So my father finally agreed to sign on today. He expected to pick up some work somewhere fairly soon after getting the push from the buses, but I think he's got the picture now. He said, "This is just until I get something else, mind," as I took him up the dole office to show him the ropes. And here comes the crappy irony, because Treorchy dole office is situated in what used to be a primary school – the one my father went to, in fact. If there is a God, like Jason thinks, I reckon He must be a cross between Ken Loach and Jeremy Beadle. It's all very well set up, but somewhat lacking in subtlety.

We decided he should declare straight away his occasional entertainment bookings. The actively seeking work part of the deal was fine, but they insisted he tells them each fortnight how much he made when he comes in. I think they deduct that much from his giro, so obviously we're not going to tell the truth. I mean, Christ, if he gets twenty quid for doing a few songs down the Non-pol he's had a particularly good night. Pissy little bits of money and pissy little lies, and I could see it was getting to him. He's always played it straight, as long as I can remember, and now he's sweating it over a tenner here and there.

Standing there by the plastic plants, watching his quiff droop over the desk, I started to wish we hadn't gone on at him so much to sign on. It's OK for me, I've done this for years, I know the routine, all the scratching and scraping and avoiding people's eyes over the vacancy boards as you pretend to be interested in a floor-sweeping job in Asda or whatever for two twenty an hour. It doesn't diminish me, all this, it's my job, how I make my living. Everybody rips each other off, snatching back a quid here, a quid there, and that goes for the employers and the social as well as us poor bastards. There's just no fucking money around, and we'll do any low thing, anything as long as it works and we can buy our packet of fags. I know some real proud, dignified bastards who do just the same as me as soon as they get in the dole office, the same petty little bullshit, the same grovelling, everything. There's what you are outside, trying to make a you-shaped dent in the world, then there's what you are when you're up the dole, a thirteen-year-old in front of the headmaster. Which is where the crappy irony of putting the dole office in a school reveals its full crappy splendour.

I say all this, get all radical and lefty, but the truth is I don't even notice it most of the time. I don't even feel any of those things. And that's my point. I don't notice it, but my Dad obviously does, because he always worked, and stood up to his bosses, and was in the union, and all that traditional Rhondda stuff. Which counts for precisely fuck all as he puts his signature at the bottom of his Job-Seeker's Agreement like he's signing a cheque for a new washing machine back in the old days when I was a kid and we went to Cardiff and came back with a car full of new stuff.

We're walking back home, then, and he asks if I've managed to sort him out any jobs, because he's getting a bit desperate. He's asked around with little success, and I've let it go lately. So I promise to try a few places later this afternoon. And back in the house he puts the kettle on and sits down grimly with his book of Top 40 hits Claire got him for his last birthday. Daytime TV burbles on about cooking and underwear and menopause difficulties, as if to remind Dad that he's not in his own world anymore, of singing along to the radio as he jokes with the boys and fixes buses. He goes through the songs, trying to expand his repertoire, not stopping to sing a few bars of the occasional song, not making up funny lyrics – just noting down the possibles in silence and sipping his tea.

I tried a few places in the afternoon but they were all booked up or not interested. In the end I caught a train back home and then Jason rang. He was in Treorchy, calling from the theatre, and very drunk. He said he was back in the play and it was great. Claire was very happy, everything was wonderful, I should hurry down and catch some real entertainment. This was about five o'clock and it had been a really miserable day, so I wasn't too enthusiastic with him. But he nagged so I went down and saw it, and then the day just sort of span right off the rails; and any hope I might have had of taking the whole thing seriously went spinning off with it. And thank fuck for that.

Jason had a letter from Claire that morning. Ticking him off for coming to Treorchy and not seeing her. Some wanky bullshit about "feeling his presence" that night. She said she knew he was in town, she could smell him, which was a bit worrying, and she didn't explain. Then, of course, Kelvin told her he'd seen him and "that explained it". She'd dropped the apology and abasement routine, thank Christ, and sounded genuinely confused. Wanted to know what he was up to, was he coming back or what. Ha ha – keep 'em guessing.

He had a shower then, sat by the plughole getting drenched, felt fucking great. Bit of a struggle getting up, as usual, and the buttons on the bastard thing were like fucking mission control, but he really loved that shower. He spent easily forty-five minutes drying, getting dressed and doing his hair. He had a bad moment when he was ready to go, sitting in his chair, about to open the front door. Just the effort, you know? The sheer bloody bother of going to the station, getting on the train, running the gauntlet of gawking turds – Christ knows he should be used to it. Down the group the other day they were talking about this. He got Martin to admit that it sometimes pisses him off when someone looks at him twice. Not very often though. His estimate was one in every twenty he wants to spit in the eye of. So that's Jason's problem, then, his ratio's wrong. There's only one in twenty that he wouldn't spit at. Fuck it, the bastards deserve it. They choose to be less than human.

He thought about Emma on the train. He wanted to go up there again, as soon as possible, and see her. He liked her flat, her pictures, her. He didn't know why – he didn't care. Like she said, there's no point wondering. Him, Phil, and Mick – they would only let go of her when they were forced to.

158

So he got to Treorchy and decided not to call on Phil yet. Wanted to psych himself up, be pure for meeting Claire. He knew she was going to a workshop at the theatre later on, so he had a few hours to get to the right type of pissed. He sat in the Red Lion on his own and read the music papers. Got lots of looks, but it was different up here because he recognised the faces. People he'd sworn at, pissed off in one way or another since he started knocking around with Phil. That was better than strangers, because they felt like old enemies, foes from the past, veterans of many an old battle. He almost felt like buying them a drink, reminiscing.

He hid by the library and watched them go in, swigging from his hip-flask to keep himself topped up. He was going to make an entrance. After Kelvin and the others went in, along came Claire. He didn't actually salivate, but she looked so good. She had her hair down, over her shoulders, and he could smell it from fifty yards away. She walked along the street, and he could feel her against his body, warm and soft. He had to fight to stay in the right mood, couldn't risk spoiling it by going weak. Some kids from her school joined her and they went in. Then some people he didn't know followed. They looked perfect – middle-aged, important, shockable. Just what he needed. So, after ten minutes, he wheeled himself down to the side door, lit a fag, and knocked three times.

Dee-Dee opened the door, her upper lip covered in cold sores, and he looked straight into the room, where they were all clustered around the desk.

"Jason," Dee-Dee said.

"Hello," Jason said, wheeling past her. "Herpes?"

Claire stared, her green eyes open wide, with her mouth open too. He gave her one of his grins, showed her he was up for a bit of mischief. Her face was a picture, he wished he could have had her reaction on video, to watch over and over.

He went right up to the big desk, reached over and flicked his fag at their ashtray. Kelvin said something welcoming, the middle-aged suits just stared.

"Right, I'm here," Jason said. "You can start now."

Philip pushed the door open and walked into the theatre. The room was empty, but he could smell the fag smoke, and a faint trace of alcohol. He sighed and walked along the corridor, up the stairs and emerged among the red plush seats. Kelvin was sitting with Dee-Dee and about six others he didn't recognise. Claire was on the stage with some of her school actors, but he couldn't see Jason.

Claire gave him a quick nod, but she was concentrating on what Kelvin and the others were saying. They didn't notice Philip, so he went up close and listened.

"An earlier version of the same character didn't work, actually," Kelvin was saying.

The middle-aged people looked sceptical about something.

"Well, what do we actually know about him?" a man asked. "He's the only one not actually connected to the school, which isn't actually a problem as such, but I think it's worth..."

"No, Brian," a woman said, "I think you're being too generous." She turned to Kelvin.

"I think you're in danger of being taken in, here, in your, your, your rush to be politically correct."

"No, no, Mrs Duncan," Kelvin said, "I can't agree, I really can't. The project is about giving a voice to people, people who rarely have that opportunity, and the point is to, kind of, listen to them, not put our words into their mouths."

"A foul mouth in his case," Mrs Duncan frowned.

"Actually, it's not the swearing as such," a man said.

"Oh, I think it is, Ted," a woman said.

"Well, yes, it is the swearing obviously," Ted said. "But it's more than that, it's the lad's actual, I mean, his whole..." he ended the sentence with a bewildered gesture.

"Yes, but that's him," Kelvin said.

"But who is he?" Mrs Duncan said.

"I just think the way he chooses to express himself is, well, unhealthy, especially for a teenage play," a woman said.

"I mean, how old is he?" Mrs Duncan asked.

Philip went to the side of the stage and nodded Claire over. "Who are they?" he said.

"One's the head and the others are governors," Claire said.

"Kelvin invited them over to watch a rehearsal."

"They picked a good night for it, then."

"He just turned up. Nobody could stop him."

"What did he do?"

"What didn't he do?"

Philip grinned and shook his head.

"Well, you asked for it," he said.

Claire cast a furtive glance at her headmaster then brought her head very close to Philip's, grinned back at him and said, "I know."

"OK, Claire," Kelvin called. "Why don't we see another scene now? We're in danger of getting a bit bogged down. I think we all need to get a bit of perspective, see things in their proper context."

"Yeah, fine," Claire said. "How about we do the rap?"

"Great, great," Kelvin nodded, and turned to the head and the governors, telling them they'd enjoy this.

Philip sat in one of the chairs and took a packet of Maltesers from his pocket. Claire disappeared into the wings, then re-appeared and stood stage left. She pressed a button on a ghetto blaster and some makeshift hip hop started booming out.

The head was tapping his foot, and Mrs Duncan smiled.

"The music was actually composed and written by pupils from the school," Kelvin said.

"That's right, that's right," Ted said, nodding.

Ben Wilmott and some others came on stage, dressed in baseball caps and big trainers, and started posing. They did a few dance steps then Ben came to the front of the stage.

"Key Stage Three, GCSE,
gotta get a good degree.
My after-school activity
makes my parents proud of me,"

he rapped, then swaggered back, letting another boy come up front,

"Gotta get an NVQ
or end up in the dole queue.

161

Don't complain, don't make a fuss,
just complete the syllabus,"

he rapped.

Philip could see the head and the governors chuckling ironically, and Kelvin nodded back at them, smiling.

A girl came to the front and rapped.

"Gotta make the grade point average,
think I need a boozy beverage
to help me through A level stress,
my social life is such a mess."

The governors were warming to it now, smiling at the kids on stage. Philip heard one of them say, "They've got a point, actually." There was an instrumental break while they did some choreographed dance steps. Claire was Philip's first warning sign. He saw her head snap up sharply as she looked off stage, into the wings. Then came a rumbling clatter, and Jason was careering across the stage, scattering the dancers.

Philip's hands went up to his face. Claire made almost exactly the same gesture.

Jason was funking it up in his chair, doing gangsta rap hand moves and slinking drunkenly around.

"Yo!" he said, making a vaguely dynamic gesture at Ben and the others. They were carrying on with the act. Jason faced the audience, said, "Yo," again, and threw a few shapes.

Philip crunched on a Malteser and cringed.

"Kick it," Jason said, in an Ice-T voice.

Kelvin stood up and stayed there, his hands flapping at his sides.

"Well, come on everybody and let's get together tonight," Jason sang. "I got diazepam in my pocket and I'm dying for a really good fight." He burped loudly, dropped the song and fell into the rap rhythm.

"I'm twenty one and I've never been shafted,
Wanna go to the doctor, get my spine regrafted."

162

He looked pleased with the rhyme, and did a victory dance. Philip noticed a whole network of rapid glances shooting between Kelvin, Claire and the ghetto blaster, but it stayed on.

"Lost in the fog, fed my dog,
went to the bog, shat a big log,
drank egg-nog, I'm just a cog,
erm, er, er, kiss my clog!"

The governors frowned.

"Michael Winner
Ate my dinner –
Cunt! Cunt! Cunt!"

Jason yelled.
Now the head stood up and Jason pointed straight at him.

"History shits on your middle-class semis!
You stifling, pebble-dashed, bed-wetting nazis!"

He burst out laughing, wheeled around and nearly knocked Ben over.

"Go on, ya bastard, breakdance!" And Jason pushed him down. Ben sprawled on the floor.

"Pathetic! I could do better," Jason said.

Kelvin was heading down the aisle to the stage, shaking his head at Claire.

Jason lurched to the side and fell right out of his chair. Philip watched him jerk and twitch on the floor, flaying the air, the veins in his neck and forehead standing out like fat blue worms.

"This is what you want, you bastards!" Jason yelled. "Look at me, I'm dancing! This is what you want," he insisted. "Especially you missus," he said in a Frankie Howerd voice, pointing at Mrs Duncan. "There's a place for us, somewhere a place for us," he sang.

Kelvin switched the ghetto blaster off and Jason stopped immediately. In complete silence he crawled to his chair, put the brakes on, grappled with the arms, tugged his upper body on the seat, grunted and turned so he was facing the right way, and finally pulled himself upright in the seat. He brushed himself down, sneered, said, "Thank you," and wheeled off stage.

Philip breathed out. No-one said a word. The silence was huge. He started applauding loudly.

"Oh, encore, encore," he cried, turning to the head and the governors. "Now that's what I call entertainment."

Claire herded her actors off the stage and into the wings, where Jason sat in the dark.

"You're a bloody nutter you are," Ben Wilmott squealed, rubbing his sore arm.

"That's showbusiness, mate," Jason said.

"I mean it, you're gone." Ben pointed at his head.

'It's called improvisation, and you're going to have to get used it if you want to make your mark in the theatre," Jason said, shaking his head sadly.

"Claire, for Christ's sake," Ben said.

"I know, I know, it'll be all right," Claire said.

"No it bloody won't, not unless he goes."

"Ben, look, we'll work something out here."

"Yeah? Like what?"

"Ben, trust me," Claire said. "There's more going on here than you know about." She looked Ben in the eyes. "Do you understand me?"

Ben looked back at her. "Well, no, not really."

Claire smiled kindly at him. "This could work out really well for us, Ben – for you and for me, you know?"

"What, this?" Ben gestured at the stage.

"Listen, Ben, we've both got the talent, and the ambition, right? But we both know what the real battle is – to be taken seriously. Am I right?"

Ben looked unsure.

"Come on, Ben – am I right?"

"Well, yeah."

She put her hand on his shoulder and lowered her voice, still

164

looking into his eyes.

"Look, we know we're not just kids playing about. But no-one else does, do they? I mean, why should they? Do you want to end up in amateur dramatics? Do you? Huh?"

"No, course not."

"Of course we don't. It's all about credibility. You know all this, we've spoken about it before."

"Yeah, but it's just...him."

"I know, I know, that wasn't fair, I know. I'll sort it. It won't happen again. Hey Ben, this isn't easy for me, either."

"No, I know it's not, I'm not saying that."

"I'm trying to get us both on here, you know?"

"Yeah, yeah, and I appreciate that, you know I do."

Claire nodded, patted Ben's shoulder. "Just trust me, and give me a chance, that's all I'm asking. OK?"

"I'm not taking shit like that again, though, Claire."

"Trust me."

Ben nodded slowly and started walking off.

"OK, OK," he said.

Claire watched him move off towards the dressing rooms, then looked down at Jason, who shook his head at her.

"You are going to be so fucking good at your job," he said, and cracked a huge smile. Her eyes lit up, she smiled and moved towards him, holding her arms out.

Philip was watching avidly as Kelvin argued with the head and the governors.

"I mean, the school's name will actually be associated with whatever comes out of all this. That's what concerns me," the head said.

"And you've had a lot of support from the school," Mrs Duncan said.

"And don't think I don't appreciate that," Kelvin said. "But this isn't about me, or the school, or, with respect, you. This is about Claire, we've had that clear from the start, it's her project."

"I'm sorry, Mr Nussbaum, I know you're an intelligent man, and I know you do a lot of good work in the community, we all know that," Mrs Duncan said. "But you're being conned here. And so is Claire. Now she's young, but you should see it happening. I'm sorry, but that's how I see it."

"Mrs Duncan, not at all, I've seen this kind of thing before, believe me, I've worked in lots of areas, and this is not uncommon. Believe me."

Mrs Duncan shook her head.

"For a lot of people," Kelvin said, "a project like this is the first time they've had the chance to let out what's inside them, so of course it's often very raw. I think Jason has the potential to make a very powerful statement, I really do. The wool is not being pulled over my eyes, really."

When they left, Kelvin sagged down into a chair, and looked at Philip.

"Heavy," Philip said.

"Ah, it's just, well... you know," Kelvin said.

"Jason's very keen to get involved," Philip said.

Kelvin nodded.

"But it has to be on his terms, you know?"

"I'm open to that," Kelvin said.

Philip sat down in the row in front of Kelvin.

"Talking of that," he said, "I've got an idea, and I wonder if you'd be interested."

"Sure, yeah, fire away," Kelvin said.

"It's my dad. He's been made redundant. I had to take him up to sign on today. It's not really his scene, y'know? He likes to be doing things. He's only got the music now, and it's not easy. You know what I mean?"

Kelvin nodded. "Yeah, I know."

"Well, I just wondered if we could perhaps get him in the play, doing some songs or whatever."

"Philip, this is a non-profit making thing."

"Yeah, I know. But it would give him something to concentrate on. Something to look forward to."

Kelvin brightened. "I think that's fine, yeah. I mean, this is the whole philosophy, if you like, behind community arts. Perhaps your father can bring some of that experience with him, add a different voice to the whole project. But, as I said, it's Claire's baby, really."

166

"She listens to you, though. Put a word in, and I'll mention it to my dad. Between us we'll prepare the ground. What do you think?"

"I'm happy to do that."

"Nice one."

Philip and Jason met up in the toilets. Jason was by the urinals when Philip walked in.

"Thank fuck for that. Give us a hand," Jason said.

"They're a bit cold."

"Hilarity makes the tears stream down my cheeks," Jason said. "Just hurry up, will you?"

Like that time by the paper recycling skip, Philip hefted Jason up from the chair, held him upright by the neck and shoulders.

"So what was the final score then?" Jason asked.

"The head and that Mrs Duncan were worried you'd give the school a bad name. Kelvin said it was down to Claire. They said she was too young to know what she was doing. Kelvin said you should stay. Stalemate at the end."

Jason chuckled. "OK, finished."

Philip eased him back into the chair and he went to wash his hands.

"So what's the plan?" Philip asked.

"No plan, Phil, I'm winging it," Jason said. "Come on, paint me a scenario."

"A scenario? OK, well, you stick with it, keep doing what you do at the rehearsals, lots of controversy but finally the play gets put on, with you in it. OK?"

"Keep going."

"Right, so you appear on stage every night for five nights, and you do something different each night. Depends what mood you're in."

"How pissed I am."

"Same thing. Kelvin gets the show on the road thanks to his arts contacts, and you perform in church halls and community centres up and down the valley. Local papers get sent the press release, someone tips them the wink about you, they send someone along. The hack can't believe her eyes. Goes backstage. She's intrigued by your charisma. Susses out something weird in the relationship between you and my sister."

"I resent that."

"Give it a year down the line, you and Claire are marginally famous. Your acidic soundbites grace the arts section of *The Western Mail*. Lots of shots of you and Claire, massively photogenic – beauty and the beast, as it were."

"Sounds great. So is this a worst-case scenario?"

"No way. Best-case. Claire gets what she wants, you get Claire. And the opportunity to shock and offend far greater numbers of people than you could manage on your own."

Jason smiled and shook his head. "I doubt it, somehow. The show probably won't get on. Either that or I'll get chucked out."

"Stranger things have happened. I wouldn't be that surprised if it went something like that."

Jason looked at Philip, saying nothing.

"What?" Philip asked.

"Where do you fit into all this?"

"This is your scenario, not mine."

"Seriously though." Jason wheeled himself closer to Philip. "What are you going to do?"

Philip shrugged. "Just wing it. Help my dad get some jobs. See Emma. Watch you offending people."

Jason was still looking at Philip. It was an uncomfortable feeling for both of them, but neither wanted to break the look yet.

"You're a right pair, you and Claire," Jason said.

Philip just smiled.

"That jacket of yours is getting a bit shabby," Jason said suddenly.

"It's all right," Philip said. "Isn't it?"

"It's getting a bit shabby. Faded. I'm going to buy you a new one."

"Yeah?"

"Yeah. Come down Cardiff next week, we'll go shopping, and I'll get you a brand new jacket."

"I prefer second-hand, really."

"We'll go to one of them funny shops in that arcade you like, then. I'll buy you a new jacket. OK?"

"Whatever you say," Philip said. "Come on, this is getting weird. They'll think we're cottaging."

Jason followed Philip out of the toilets.

"You shouldn't be afraid of your sexuality, you know Phil."

"It's yours I'm afraid of."

Jason laughed. "Yeah, I'm not fussy, I'll have anything."

He made a lunge for Philip's arse. Philip laughed and jumped out of the way, spinning around to punch Jason in the stomach.

"Piss off, you bummer."

"Don't be so repressed."

They scuffled around in the corridor and, pausing for breath, found Claire watching them.

"Boys never really grow up, do they?" she said.

12. NOVEMBER 1993.

It was one of those nights when the valley seemed alive to Philip. It was Friday, that helped. And it was quite mild, so as he walked from his house down to Pentre, Philip saw people everywhere. About thirty kids were hanging around outside Spar, identical with their crew cuts and black bomber jackets. A large woman in pink ski-pants picked her way through them, muttering under her breath.

In his big, black boots Philip strode down the main street, smoking a cigarette. A big thick-set man with spiky hair got out of a car, walked into Philip's path. He side-stepped the man, making sure he had a half-smile on his lips and carried on down the street. It had been a stupid hobby, but it helped you walk tall.

His father had seemed pretty pleased about getting the gig in Claire's play. He was going to do *Summertime Blues*, *Travelling Light*, *Can't Buy Me Love* and *Simply the Best*. People went out for a good time, he said, to get away from their problems. So he was going to encourage them to sing along. Philip couldn't wait to see the finished play. Between one thing and another it would have McKay stamped right the way through it. He smirked, and kept walking.

When he got to The Railway he saw Minty over in the corner, but didn't flinch. He'd got away with it, he was home and dry. He even half-smiled as he went up to the bar and asked for Mike the landlord.

"Do you ever have entertainment on?" Philip asked. "Only my dad plays guitar and sings, and he's available for bookings."

"Nah, we do have a disco here on Thursdays and Saturdays, like," Mike said, "but other than that we don't bother."

"He's pretty good."

"Aye, I'm not doubting that he's good, like. It's just not our kind of thing."

Philip frowned. The Railway was a bit of a long shot

anyway. But he was running out of pubs at the top end of the valley.

"How about just one night, as a trial, see how it goes, like?" Philip said.

"Well," Mike said, flicking ash from his cigar and glancing at his barmaid's arse. "What sort of music do he do, like?"

"Oh Christ, all sorts. Modern stuff too, you know."

"Aye, like what?"

"Queen. Elton John. He does that Bryan Adams song. That goes down well."

"Nah, it's not our kind of thing. We do get a younger crowd in here."

Yeah, as in under-age; well, fuck you and your drug-den, Philip wanted to say, but he just shrugged and said, "Fair enough." Mike went to serve someone and Philip knocked back his whiskey. Then there was someone on either side of him, pressing in close.

"Walk outside," Corky said.

"Now," Lufty said.

Philip could suddenly feel the pulse beating in his neck. It was making him feel sick. A sharp pain dug into his ribs.

"Now," Corky said.

The only chance was to do what they said then make a run for it outside. He thought about this, about running. The fucking fags, that was the problem. He would die if he had to run more than two hundred yards at full speed. He slowly turned away from the bar and started walking down to the door. Corky and Lufty were just behind him, on his right and left. His elbows brushed up against their arms as they walked.

Philip opened the door of the pub and took off. Something opened up in his brain, a gear change, and he was off. This was it. He got less than ten feet when they crashed on him. He didn't quite fall to the ground but their weight dragged him to a dead stop.

"Up here, fucker," Corky said.

They pushed and shoved him around the back of the pub, past the security light and into the dark. He couldn't see a thing, but there was a strong smell of engine oil. He tripped over something which clanged. It might have been an exhaust pipe.

They stopped and stood there.

"Look, I haven't done anything, you've got the wrong bloke," Philip said.

"Where's your mate?" Corky said.

"Jason?"

"Mick," Lufty said.

"I don't know. I haven't seen him. I don't know what this is all about. Just let me go, like, is it? I'm no trouble."

Philip felt as though he'd taken speed. His mind was weighing everything up at a hundred miles an hour. He'd had both their girlfriends. It could be that. They'd kill him. But they were asking about Mick, so it could be something else. Something to do with drugs. If it was that, it really wasn't to do with him, and perhaps he could get out of it.

"I don't know anything about Mick. I don't bother with him that much. I don't really know him."

There was another sharp pain in his ribs, and he looked down at Corky's knife.

Something else opened up in him, another gear change. The machinery was screaming.

"Look. I don't know –"

Lufty punched him three times in the head, but Philip saw it coming and covered himself. The blows bounced off, so Lufty gave him an angry punch in the stomach. Philip doubled up, gasping. Corky laid into him, punching his head and face as he staggered around. Even now, Philip was working out the angles, and even realising he was doing it. If he kept himself protected he could take a fair bit of this. Perhaps they'd get bored after a while. He took another easy punch to the stomach but stumbled over the exhaust pipe and fell on the floor.

"Hang on, hang on!" he shouted, not knowing why.

They started kicking him, and he rolled from side to side, trying to avoid their trainers. They stopped then, and stood back. He knew better than to get up straight away, and tried to act more hurt than he was, reeling around on his haunches. They might decide then that he had had enough.

Panting, Philip looked up at them and said, "Look, honest

to God, I don't know anything, I'll fuck off, honest to God, you won't see me again."

They were both still, so he decided to risk getting up. Perhaps they would let him go.

"I don't want no trouble, honest to God, I'll fuck off," he said, staggering to his feet.

Corky punched him in the eye. Unprotected. There was an explosion in his head. Pain burst from his eye, streaked across his face. He cried out and fell on the floor, his hands clutching for a something to hold. He landed hard on his hip and cried out again.

"You fucker," Corky jeered.

All thoughts were gone. He rolled around, trying to deal with the pain, trying to breathe. Someone was coming, he could see through one eye, a shadow. Corky and Lufty looked around. Thank fuck. The figure walked up to Philip and looked at him. Squinting up into the dark, his hand pressed to his eye, Philip saw who it was.

"All right, mate?" Minty said.

A bowling ball fell into Philip's stomach, forcing everything down.

Minty chuckled at Corky and Lufty, who chuckled back. Then he unzipped his jeans and stood there. Philip lay where he was, and heard the noises of the street echoing from the front of the pub; laughter and shouts, cars speeding off. The hot stream of Minty's piss splashed on to his jacket, and he retched, closed his other eye. They were laughing, the three of them.

When he had emptied his bladder, Minty zipped up and set off back to the pub.

"Tell Mick what we told you," Corky said.

"The fucker," Lufty added, and they went.

Philip sat up, shivered, and started digging through his pockets for his fags. They were soaked.

"Oh, piss," Jason said.

"What's the matter?" Claire said.

"I've just wheeled over something."

"What is it?"

173

Jason looked down at the pavement.

"It looks like a rissole."

"Oh, that's going to get all over your tyre."

"It already has."

They got to the house and Claire went in to get a fork. In the kitchen was a partially dismembered washing machine. Val was digging around in its guts with a voltmeter. Joan had to step over him to make herself a cup of coffee.

"Hello," Claire said.

"Hiya, love," Val said.

"What's going on?" Claire stepped over a bundle of wires to the cutlery drawer.

"I'm having a look at this for a mate of mine. The motor's cutting out."

"I said he'd be better off with a service man," Joan said.

"No, it's all electrics, isn't it?" Val said, leaning on one elbow. "Might be worth looking into, I thought, you know, doing repairs. It's all electrics, like, it's not that much different to what I was doing."

"Where are you going with that fork?" Joan said.

"Jason's got rissole on his tyre."

"How did the rehearsal go?" Val said.

"All right, it's coming along."

"I'll have to come down there one day, familiarise myself with the set-up. The PA and that."

"Yeah, come down," Claire said. "Is Philip in?"

"No, he went out. He's trying to get me some jobs. I think he went down The Railway."

Claire went back out and she and Jason started digging the rissole out from the tracks of his tyre. They heard the phone ring, then Joan called to them.

"It's someone called Mick. He wants to talk to Jason."

"But I'll get rissole on the carpet," Jason said.

Claire smiled and kissed his cheek. "Who is he?"

"Mate of Philip's."

"I'll go and see what he wants."

Jason sat in his chair on the doorstep with the fork in his left hand, looking up and down the street. He realised that he wasn't in the least bit annoyed about the rissole, about having to sit out here. Some option was forming itself quietly, some new form, and it was so tempting. It was like a new version of himself, Jason mark two. It was like a deep sea, where all was calm, but you knew better than to take chances with it. It had storms and tsunami waves, but it also had trenches and reefs and everything else. You couldn't argue with the sea, it just was. A quiet relief was sneaking into him, and he had to be still to appreciate its unfamiliar texture – and the being still was part of it.

Claire came rushing out of the house.

"Phil's been beaten up," she said.

They went to the Con Club, where Mick and Philip were sitting on the steps. Philip's left eye was swollen shut and his face was bloody.

"He's all wet," Jason said.

"It's piss," Mick said. "They had a piss on him."

"Are you OK?" Claire said, looking into her brother's face.

"Could be worse," Philip said, shivering. "I'm freezing cold. Can you get me some clothes? I'm going up Emma's."

"Phil, wise up, you only live around the corner," Jason said. "Come home and we'll get you sorted."

"Home is where the heart is," Mick nodded.

"No, I want to go up Emma's," he said. "Sit in front of the fire."

Mick, Jason and Claire exchanged glances, then looked back at Philip.

"I'll get you clothes, but where are you going to change?" Claire said.

"I hadn't considered the logistics."

They got him into and out of the house without Val or Joan noticing. Then the four of them set off up the road. Philip was limping and breathing heavily.

"This really isn't a good idea," Claire said. "What's wrong with your leg?"

"I fell on my hip," Philip said. "Right on the bone."

"Look, let's go back to the house," Claire said.

"She's right, mate," Mick said. "It's many, many miles to Emma's."

But they kept going, until Philip had to stop and sit down.

"Oh fuck, I can't go any further," he said.

"Phil, it's just as far back as forward now," Claire said.

"It kills," Philip said, rubbing his hip.

Jason looked up and down the road, followed some speeding cars with his eyes, then looked at Philip.

"Right, come on," he said, and hurried off down a side street.

The others followed, Philip hobbling along.

"Put him on me," Jason said.

"What?" Philip said.

"Sideways, across the arms," Jason said.

"Jase, look," Philip said.

"We'll be here all night. Now come on."

Claire and Mick helped Philip on to the chair. He was lying sideways across Jason.

"I feel like an idiot," he said.

"Well we'll go up the back roads," Claire said.

"Yeah, if anyone sees they'll just think Jason's got one of them clip-on tables," Mick said.

Claire gave him a strange look.

"Come on, let's go," Jason said.

"I'll push," Claire said.

"I can manage," Jason said, and reached under Philip's legs and back to start wheeling the chair forward. "He weighs about as much as a plastic fork."

They moved off down the side street.

Emma was sitting by her window, reading a magazine. She looked up, saw them, and opened the front door.

"What the hell's happened?" she said.

"Philip's had a bit of a kicking," Mick said. "It's not as bad as it looks, though. Unless there's internal bleeding."

They all looked at him.

"I don't think there is though," Mick said. "He's just a bit pissy. We've got dry clothes for him though."

They went through to the living room, Claire looking around with wide eyes.

"This is Claire," Jason said, looking for somewhere to off-load Philip. "Remember I was telling you about her?"

Emma nodded and moved some videos and books off the settee.

"Put him down here."

They helped him lie down then stood back.

"Who was it?" Emma said.

"Corky and somebody else," Philip said. "Can't remember his name. Then Minty came along."

"Minty?" Emma said.

"Yeah. He pissed over me."

"You're lucky that's all he did."

"I know. Believe me, I was grateful for every last drop."

Emma shook her head, knelt and looked at Philip's swollen eye.

"Oh, you silly fucker," she said.

"I didn't do nothing. They wanted Mick."

Emma turned on Mick, who shifted from foot to foot.

"Don't look at me. I didn't do nothing neither, I don't know what all this is about, like,"

"You're both as bad as each other," Emma said, "buggering about all the time."

"I don't suppose I've helped either," Jason mumbled.

Everyone stared at him, even Philip. Jason just shrugged.

"Yeah, well, that's all bloody finished now," Philip said. "That's me out of it. I'm keeping my bastard head down from now on."

"About time," Claire said.

They had just started to relax when they heard a car pull up outside. They looked at each other, a network of glances, Claire to Jason, him to Philip, Phil to Mick, Mick to Emma, Emma to the front door, from which a knocking now came.

"Wait here. Quiet," Emma said.

"Oh fuck," Mick said, scratching his head.

Jason began clenching and unclenching his fists, staring at the door like a dog.

They heard voices, then Emma speaking firmly. There was a pause, some more talking, then finally footsteps, the front door closing, the car's ignition. Emma returned. They were all looking up at her: Philip out of one eye, lying flat out on her settee, his boots dangling over the end; Jason next to him, partly obscuring him, his shoulders tense and hunched; Mick by the fire, his misshapen shadow flickering on the wall; and Claire standing at the end of the settee, looking so young, her green eyes open wide.

"Corky and Lufty," Emma told them. "With their girl-friends. Wanted to come in for five." She watched the four of them breathe out, drop their heads and look up at her again. Then she looked at her watch. "The pubs have shut." She giggled. "But I think I've got enough people in here for one night."

A BRUSH WITH DEATH.

Remember that bit in *Lucky Jim* where he burns a hole in the bed sheets? Well, apparently I've done the same to a continental quilt belonging to the valley's most influential drug dealer, and I risk more than social disgrace if I'm caught.

This was in the aftermath of shagging his girlfriend, of course, and she wants me to buy a new duvet or I'm in trouble. She could be bluffing, but all the same I'm off to Argos tomorrow.

Affecting an air of nonchalance in one's journals is all very well, but I was actually cakking it, big time. Of all the stupid, pointless things I've done, this was absolutely, definitively the stupidest, the most pointless, the ultimate howl into the largely self-created void, if you see what I mean.

Look, you've got pride, right? Dignity and self-respect. That whole package. Well, I've always thought of all that as a fairly bogus set of concepts, a flawed paradigm. Some bloke accidentally spills your pint, to take the classic example, so you ram the glass into his face. Why? Pride. Dignity. Self-respect. I admit I'm generalising, but not wildly I don't think.

I was immune to all that. Christ, until I was sixteen I thought I lived in a suburb. I thought I was middle class, like in *The Good Life* or whatever. But roots are roots, I suppose – how else to explain what I did?

So, I was licking my wounds, mostly at Emma's house. Jason and Claire were there a lot as well, usually after rehearsals. They're trying to keep it away from our parents, which is probably for the best. I think Claire enjoys being ambiguous about it all, but I don't worry about Jason now. He knows how to handle her, if you'll excuse the sickening innuendo. Anyway, I just sat around Emma's place, and I kept thinking about things, and I got very twitchy every time I heard a noise outside. Mick has been lying low too. He claims to have no idea what it was all about. But it just kept going through my head, Minty pissing on me more than anything, and how unfair it was that I'd beaten them all, had all their girlfriends, for months, but he could still just piss on me, because I couldn't gloat about my victory. Of course, he'd have stabbed me if I had told him, but in my fevered brain that seemed a better thing than being pissed on. Hence all this dignity crap. I couldn't get it out of my system. Things were just coming nice, with Jason and Claire all mellow and having fun, and Mick and Emma and me just chilling up the flat. But it was just too neat for me to resist. That's another explanation, I suppose. Number two seed.

Just one bird I hadn't fucked and she was Minty's. It would seem wrong to ignore such neat plotting. I felt as though all of us – all five of us – had our parts to play, and this was mine. After that was over, who knew?

Minty was out of town, on another mission. I'd already spoken to his girlfriend a few times. The ground was far from fallow, as per bloody usual. I'll spare you the details and cut to the chase.

My pupils must have been like fucking dinner plates, between the pinch of speed and the natural adrenalin flow inspired by the occasion. It was during the sweet post-coital fag that she dropped the bombshell – Minty was coming back that night. In the circumstances I think I can be excused an inadvertent cigarette burn. She's lucky I didn't burn the whole fucking house down. It seemed inconceivable that she could be so recklessly stupid – he'd kill her too, obviously – but then she was tamazied to the tits.

So I grabbed my clothes and got ready to do the scalded cat routine through the cluttered house, trying to tune out my heartbeat and listen for Minty's BMW. It was weird how much I knew about him. I don't think he even knew my name. Unless he thought my mother had actually christened me Cunt.

There were obstacles everywhere, trying to bring me down. Minty had televisions and videos all over the house. Stereos too and even computers. If I fell, it was all over. Minty would be on me, and I'd have to explain why, for the last twelve months, I'd been screwing every girl in town, every last one of Minty's harem, culminating tonight with his fucking fiancée. Trying to explain would be worse than the violence.

Ripped leather sofa to my left. I couldn't slow down to dodge it, so I went right over. I landed badly, stumbled on a load of CDs, got up and opened the hallway door. It was the wrong door, I was in the living room. More of Minty's girls, sprawled around, must have come in while I was upstairs, listening to reggae. They looked up at me, all dopey eyes and huge gold necklaces. I span around, jerked the door open and a baseball cap suddenly cut through the dark at me.

"Right between the tits!"

This was Minty's cry as he hit me. For a second after the door opened, we grinned at each other. Our lives were descending into farce, mine and Minty's. Someone had to make a stand. It was him. A sharp little fist to the chest and I went backwards over the coffee table, crashing down in a shower of fag ash and blow. The girls were pissed off. I'd broken a CD case. I had a weird flash in my mind at that point: my bookshelves at home, with all my books, in alphabetical order from Anouilh to Zola, all waiting for me to come home.

I shook my head and sped off around the room. There was not real plan, just keep moving and hope I could dodge to the door. I did a quick lap of the room then bolted for it. Minty, strangely, took his attention off me for that second, doing something with the girls. I couldn't imagine what would be more important to him than getting his hands on me at that point.

I was out on the street, running along the estate, looking for the dark edges where the streets met the mountain, where Minty's car couldn't follow. Minty didn't run anywhere. The BMW was already revving up, spotlighting me in the headlights. Somewhere along the line I had made the wrong decision, made some kind of mistake, and this is where it led. It was before I even started shagging the girls, before I even left school. It seemed to be Jason, and I wished he was here with me now, running along with me, ready to take Minty on for me.

I went down an alley, surfaced in another, identical street, heard Minty's car roar. This was the clever bit. I had a plan now. I'd rehearsed it in my head all those bruised weeks, but never thought I might have to use it. Almost forgotten, but now it was back, in detail. Minty would come around the bend and pull into Glenroy Street, where I was now. But by this time I would be on my way back up the alley I'd just come down, emerging back in Oakland Crescent, and I'd leg it to Minty's house. By the time he got wise and brought the car back around, I would have hurtled right through his house, out the back door and into the garden, over the fence and away. Minty's was the last street before the mountain. I could lose myself in the undergrowth, then just keep heading up the mountain. Just keep going, maybe come down in the Lake District at the age of forty, safe at last.

I came to his front door. He'd closed it after him. I was rather surprised he'd bothered. So I hammered on it, hearing his engine echoing around the estate, until one of the girls opened up. I pushed past her – realising with a little shock I'd shagged her – and headed for the back door.

I was plunging into the pitch black then, propelled by a huge leap from his fence, my feet springing up and down in the marshy ground. And the dark closed around me, and a fresh vat of adrenalin or fear up-ended itself inside me. If he came up here, it really was over. I wouldn't have time to explain anything to him. The streets are one thing, the narrow, curving towns where we're all crammed in and have to live. But that's just a narrow slit and on either side the darkness looms, unknown acres of it. There are only a few reasons for going into it. Sex is one. Violence is another. Nature rambles are a third.

I kept going, up and up the valley wall. After about twenty minutes I was in the forest. I couldn't see anything but slices of sky, a shade lighter than the mountain, high above me.

When I was above the treeline, I looked down at the estate. Something was going on. Noises were echoing up to me, engines revving, voices. Then a siren. Oh shit. Whenever the police get involved, everything always gets ten times worse than it was before.

I started scrambling up the mountain again, my boots dislodging rocks now instead of grass and ferns. Gasping, spitting what felt like major organs, I reached a big fat outcrop sticking out from the summit. There was nothing above me but indigo sky now. I looked down again, right over the top of the trees and allotments. Two police cars and a van, it looked like, were driving away down the street, their blue lights strobing the estate.

I dared to hope – could I be that lucky? Would the cops have taken Minty off tonight of all nights, when he'd been building his business up for years right under their noses, and by doing so save my skinny life? And they say there's never one around when you need one.

So I spent the night on the mountain, scared to come down, and nearly froze to death. It was about three when I got up there, and I spent the time until dawn warming my fingers over my lighter flame. At around five, gazing down into the valley, the orange streetlights glowing up at me, I became convinced I was God, peering down into Hell.

Then I fell asleep for about half an hour. I woke, had a quick vomit, examined the imprint of Minty's signet ring on my chest, and started off down the mountain.

I spent the next day hiding at home, but I had to know what happened to Minty. So I went to The Red Lion with my dad, who still has his regular Saturday slot there. And I met a friend of the girl whose quilt I'd damaged. Minty was in Swansea nick, having been just that bit too casual in his dealings. You know how rare it is that they catch a dealer, and he was looking at five to ten. She told me, I thanked her, then went to the toilet. I felt the need to vomit again.

I knew it couldn't have been God that arranged this, because He wouldn't have been interested in my case. So I just offered silent thanks to whoever was the author of this particular *deus ex machina*. And that really is it for me, now. I'm announcing my retirement. If you think about it, I should get a mention in the local paper. Never mind your bronze medal athletes from Blaencwm, or tenth-rate actors who lived here for a few months in 1974. I deserve some serious recognition here. Yes, it was stupid, suicidal and lacking in a basic moral structure to underpin my unbelievable courage, but the same is true of mountaineering, or any other so-called dangerous sport.

I'm going up Emma's house tonight. I'm not going to tell any of them what happened. What's the point? It's all over now.

That was the good news anyway. The not so good news is that Minty's girlfriend has, in the way of these things, immediately taken up with the Rhondda's second most influential dealer. Which, she reckons, is worth a new duvet. And I have to agree.

13. DECEMBER/JANUARY 1994.

"Thing is," Mick said, "I'd have thought he'd only been, like, disabled for a while, you know, a couple of years."

"No," Philip said, "he's a paraplegic. He's always been like it."

Mick nodded thoughtfully and picked up his pint. "The reason I'm thinking along those lines, like, is because, y'know, how pissed off he is about it. I'd have thought he'd have had plenty of time to get used to it by now."

"I wouldn't say that to him, Mick," Philip said. "He hates that. It's like, he says it's the whole point. Getting used to things. He doesn't care if it happened yesterday or if it's been around forever. He's either for it or against it."

"I can see his point, man. Seriously, I often feel quite similar." He nodded slowly. "Very fucking similar indeed, if you want to know the truth." He was still nodding his head, his eyes a bit glazed. He'd smoked an obese spliff in the toilets a few minutes earlier.

Philip looked up at his father, who was switching his mike back on after his break. The funny thing was that now he was no longer doing this for fun, he looked every inch the professional. It was the slightly jaded look in his eyes as he cued up the tape machine, the calculating glance at the audience. He still sounded like an amateur, though. He started doing an Everly Brothers number.

"But the thing is," Mick said, pointing at Philip, "is this: you've got to, like, present yourself, regardless of the kind of..." he shook his head. "The fucking unbearable bastard smugness, you know, the bloody grinning, you know, the grinning insect-faced bastardness of it all," he said frowning. "Despite all that, you know, you got to sort of swim like one of them fish. What are they called?"

"Trout?"

"Smaller."

"Minnows."

"No," Mick said. "Yeah. Actually, yeah. You've got to be a minnow."

He started doing minnow movements with his hands to demonstrate. A woman on her way back to the table, laden with drinks, scowled at Mick.

"Chill, babe, I'm in discussion," Mick drawled.

Philip threw back his head and laughed. Nutters, he thought, always the nutters, always sitting in pubs with nutters being embarrassing. He was a fucking glutton for it.

"I need to express to Jason my deep understanding of his problems, you know?" Mick said. "I'm on his side, I was born wrong too, with me?"

Philip nodded.

"But I've got to communicate with him what I've discovered about the essential, y'know, the facts of the matter, which is, basically, that he's got to chill, stop burning all his propane gas, if you see what I mean, and find some little..." he wiggled his hands around.

"Y'know?" he said.

"Yeah, Mick, I know what you're saying."

"Do you?" He looked surprised. "Then you must tell him. He's more likely to accept the truth of it through you."

"To be honest, Mick, I think he's starting to get the picture himself."

Mick clapped a hand over his mouth. "I'll say no more, then."

He stayed like that for a while, until his eyes started rolling, and he mumbled, "Well, I will, obviously."

Philip burst out laughing.

"Let's finish these and go up Emma's place," Mick said.

Philip nodded and said, "So what do you think of my dad then?"

Mick cocked his head sideways, twisting his blunt shoulders at Val. He closed his eyes and his forehead wrinkled.

Val sang the word "dream", trying to mimic the elastic vowels of the Everlys, gasping a lungful of air before the next line.

"He's class," Mick said. "That's the real thing that is – you can hear it. You know? Like Tom Waits or whatever, y'know, Beefheart."

186

Philip laughed, then jumped as Mick suddenly kissed him on the cheek.

"Friends should be friends," Mick said, then he shouted, "Yeah!" He drained his pint and got up. "I gotta piss," he said and stumbled across the room.

Jason was up at Emma's place, drinking red wine with her.

"I thought it would be a bit of a change, that's why I asked you to get it," Emma said.

Jason nodded, sipping the wine. "Smoother than my normal tipple," he said.

"How was the rehearsal?"

"Oh, I didn't do anything on this occasion. Just sat and watched. Made a few comments. It's all bollocks really, isn't it?" He looked to Emma, but she just shrugged.

"You never bloody agree, do you?"

She shrugged again, and they laughed.

"Seriously," Jason said. "Do you think I should carry on with it, or pack it in?"

Emma was quiet for a minute. Jason watched her rub her eye, adjust her ankh, massage her neck and settle into a more comfortable position. He was about to say something when she answered him.

"Like you say, it's all bollocks, so you might as well do it."

"I think the opposite: it's all bollocks so what's the point?"

She sighed, and when she spoke again sounded quite annoyed. "What's the point of anything? Just fucking well do it, make a big fuss, piss everyone off, look good to Claire. Why not?"

"It's so fucking ... nothing," Jason said, and his voice was a bit whiny. "It's not real, is it? It doesn't add up to anything."

"Fuck all adds up to anything," Emma said, impatiently. "You know that, for fuck's sake. Wise up, Jason, you can't do fuck all. You might as well make yourself look like a tit. It's all the bastard same."

Jason nodded his head, gazed into the fire. Emma watched him for a few minutes, then suddenly shook her head and went to fetch a felt tip pen. He watched her, still frowning, as she came up to him with a hard look in her eyes, and started to draw on his face.

"Emma! Get off, you mad cow! Jesus!"

She was grinning now, an evil little smile, as she fought him, and started drawing a smiley face on his real, pensive one. He wasn't seriously fighting anymore – he was laughing too much. When she finished, Emma stood back and looked at him.

"See? Much better," she said, smiling like an eight-year-old.

She took another step back, onto an ashtray, and fag ends spilled everywhere.

"Bollocks."

Jason laughed and pointed at her, making triumphant noises. Emma scowled, then started singing the theme tune to a kids' TV programme at him, trying to drown him out. They stopped suddenly, hearing footsteps outside. Noisy and drunk, bumping into bins. Emma held a finger to her lips, dead serious. They listened, and heard muffled voices.

"...was in one episode of *The Six Million Dollar Man*."

"Bullshit."

"Serious. On my cat's life."

"Fuck your cat, Mick."

"That's a bit harsh."

"Nah, fuck it. Cary Grant was never in..."

"He fucking was!"

Jason relaxed. "It's just the kids."

"Better let them in," Emma said. "Before the idiots get arrested."

Jason thought about that episode of *Casualty*, all that time ago, spilling it all out to Phil in that stifling hot living room in Newport. It got him so pissed off at the time, made it all look so easy. And now here he was in a reasonable facsimile of that gang of friends. Whether it was God or the author, some such crappy conceit, you had to admire the fucking sense of humour. No, just understand it. And he understood it all right. The dance went on, it's all there was. Optimism was not the point. Being suave was, whatever it cost.

Emma opened the front door and Philip and Mick staggered in.

"Emma, babes," Mick said, trying to kiss her.

"You two treat this place like a hotel," she said.

Phil and Mick fell into the living room, smelling of fags and booze and cold night-time air. Jason turned slowly in his chair, and lifted his glass of wine to them, his felt-pen eyebrows and mouth offering them a welcoming smile.

"Gentlemen, good evening. How nice of you to come," he said, and dissolved into giggles.

On the first day of the new year, just after one in the afternoon, Jason woke up and coughed. Claire's head, on his chest, stirred then was still. Jason closed his eyes as his head started to pound, then he opened them and looked around the room. The windows were frost-laced, and a piercing light shone through, now the council had taken the metal off.

His back was aching. Claire's weight didn't help. Strands of her hair tickled his nose. He also wanted a piss. But he stayed still for as long as he could, looking down at Claire, not wanting to move. In the end he started to get up, looking for his clothes. She opened her eyes to look at him, smiled sleepily, then curled up into a tight ball, drawing the quilt over her. Jason grinned, rubbing the cramp out of his spine, squinting at Claire through sleep-watery eyes.

In the kitchen he found Phil, making tea.

"Morning," Phil said. His voice was hoarse. "Want one?"

"I'll have a coffee."

Philip was wearing jogging trousers and several jumpers, curled around his hands like gloves. Over the top he wore a huge black shirt with the top of a fag packet peeping out from the pocket. His breath steamed out in front of him.

"What happened with Mick?" Jason said.

"Ah, he came back eventually. That speed must have been a bit strong. We think he ran all the way down to Spar. When he came back he was wrecked, and he fell asleep straight away. Funny thing was, he was carrying a big road sign above his head."

"What?"

"We put it out there."

Jason peered out into the passage where a large metal sign was propped against the wall.

"Works Access Only" Jason read.

"It weighs a ton." Phil poured hot water into their cups, spilling some on the washing machine he used as a work surface. "He must be really strong."

"I bet he does use those weights," Jason said, rubbing his chin.

Phil nodded, yawned, and handed Jason his coffee.

"There was snow in the night. After you'd all gone to bed. Me and Emma watched it out the window," Phil said.

Jason pulled back the roller blind and looked out. A few inches lay over everything, softening the estate's pointed edges. Over the other side of the valley, the peak was white and flecked, looking higher than usual.

"Looks all right in the snow, don't it?" Phil said.

Jason nodded, gazing out, gently dazzled by the snow's luminescence. It was quiet in the kitchen, without even a distant car's engine thrum.

"Nightmare to get around in," Jason said, still gazing out.

"Wait till it melts," Phil said. His face too was turned to the window. "That's when the trouble'll start. Slush all over the place."

"Yeah." Jason nodded. "The kerbs." He looked at Phil.

"When all the people go back to work in their cars," Phil said, "it'll all be dirty and brown and splash all over you."

They drank quietly for a few minutes, lighting up fags, coughing and spluttering then grinning at each other.

"Claire OK?" Phil said.

"Still asleep."

Jason noticed how creased his friend's face looked in the snowbright kitchen. His eye hadn't really come right after he was hit that time. It didn't seem to open as wide as the other one. But no-one would really notice, not unless they knew Phil like he did.

"Got to remember to get Emma's Lottery tickets today," Phil said. "Have to go down the shop later."

"Is it open today?"

"Yeah, there was a sign on it, with the apostrophe in the wrong place."

"What?"

"New Year's Day. The apostrophe was after the s."

Jason giggled. "You tosser."

Phil stuck two fingers up.

"Actually, I owe her a bottle of vodka as well," Jason said.

"Let's go and see if they're awake," Phil said.

They followed the trail of Silly String along the walls to the living room. Claire passed them on the way to the bathroom.

"Don't look," she said, covering her face. "I look like poo." She disappeared into the bathroom and they heard water running. Then her head popped back out. "Jase, I can't stay long, I've got loads of coursework to do, and I've only got eight days to do it in."

"Piece of piss." Jason smiled as she blew him a kiss, and the bathroom door closed again.

They went into the living room, which smelt of cigarette smoke and Chinese food. They saw Mick, his hunched little body spread-eagled in an armchair. He had two artificial eyebrows made of Silly String.

"It seemed funny at the time," Phil said.

"I bet it did."

Emma was in her usual position, upside down in the armchair. Her first view when she opened her eyes would be her wall of pictures, rising up and up. Jason picked up a poker and started prodding at what was left of the fire.

Philip sat on the floor, leaning against Emma's armchair. He could feel her warmth against his shoulder. He closed his eyes, and he could hear Jason stabbing and crunching at the fire, Mick snoring, hot water running through the pipes as Claire washed her face.

He thought about going out, about the prints his boots would make in the snow. He wanted everyone to come out, into the back garden, and make prints: Claire's trainers, Jason's wheels, Mick's Docs, Emma's shoes. He wanted them all to make their prints before it started to melt, or get dirty. While it was still bright and white. He got up and went over to Jason.

"Let's wake them up," he said.

"Yeah, in a minute," Jason said. Then he reached into the pocket of Philip's shirt and took out his packet of cigarettes. "But let's have a quiet fag first, you and me, yeah?"

"Why not?" Philip smiled, and let Jason light him a cigarette.